Lies Beyond The Altar

Parris Iris

Published by Parris Iris, 2024.

LIES BEYOND THE ALTAR

First edition. August 31, 2024.

ISBN: 979-8227094803

Written by Parris Iris.

Dedication

To my Lord and Savior, thank you for the early morning prayer sessions in which you encouraged me to *write the vision and make it plain (Habakkuk 2:2)*

To my children, you have always been my inspiration. Because of God and the three of you, I have been able to write my first book. I would put the manuscript on the bookshelf to complete later, but the three of you ensured I kept writing. Thank you for the trips to the beach that allowed me to clear my head and keep on writing.

To my mother, sister, and sisters-in-law the women in my life who have always questioned what I am doing now—well, now you know.

To my nieces who always think Auntie can do anything! When I wasn't answering the phone, I was writing.

To my GINA GINA, thank you for your daily prayers, reminding me that all things are possible with God.

To my brothers and brother-in-law, thank you for protecting me and helping me understand men—although you all still confuse me.

To my dad! I miss you with every beat of my heart. I love you so very much. You are the dad who provided without hesitation. I did not always understand your sternness until I became an adult and a mother. I appreciate God for lending you to me for the time I had you. You were my encouragement, listening ear, architect, carpenter instructor, etc...

PROLOGUE

I sit here on the sofa, bewildered, wondering what happened. The TV is on, but I cannot tell you what is happening with this show because my tears won't stop falling as I focus on my life's turn of events. I am usually not a spirits drinker, but today may be a good day to start. I get up and find an ABC Package Store. I wipe the tears and put on my bright smile, which I have been told lights up a room. What a beautiful job two rounds of braces and twice-per-year visits to the dentist for cleaning will do.

I walked in and became overwhelmed by what was in front of me. There were aisles and aisles of what may help with the thoughts that would not stop circulating in my head. I've been perusing the aisles, trying to avoid eye contact with anyone. I did not want to engage in conversation right now. I am trying to find whatever I am looking for, even though I have no idea what it is. I want to complete my purchase and get back home, especially since COVID-19 is still running rampant across the globe.

I caught the eye of a young man who appeared too young to work in a liquor store. He did not look over eighteen years old; eighteen was generous because he looked about sixteen. He asked me if I needed help with anything. I told him I was looking for a sweet, fruity drink that would allow me to clear my head. He began telling me that Lobos 1707 Reposado tequila would be good. I interrupted him and asked if he was old enough to advise me on alcoholic beverages. He said yes, ma'am, I am old enough. I am twenty-two years old and have graduated from the oldest HBCU in North Carolina. I asked him why he worked at a package store if he had graduated from college. He quickly advised me that he had accepted this position while awaiting an acceptance letter from a corporation he had interviewed with. Also, this job offers a pension, and not many companies provide pensions. This young man was more aware of retirement than I was.

I almost forgot about my issues as I conversed more with this young man. He was highly attentive, articulate, polite, and helpful. So, what college did you graduate from? Johnson C. Smith University, he proudly stated. I am no expert on HBCUs, but Johnson C. Smith does not sound like a Historically Black College and University. He gave me some information about JCSU's history, informing me that JCSU is located on Beatties Ford Rd. in Charlotte, was founded in 1867, and was one of the oldest HBCUs in North Carolina. That's the HBCU on the Ford, the sketchy area of town you never visit unless you were invited. After grilling this young man on his knowledge, he showed me where the tequila was.

Should I just put the tequila in a glass or mix it with something? You can add juice or have it over ice. Whichever way you decide to have it, make sure to sip it. Do not guzzle it. As he and I walked to the front of the store so that I could check out, he told me about a drink called the Lobos Swizzle. He handed me one of the drink recipe cards at the front of the store. I glanced over the card and needed two ounces of tequila, ½ ounce of fresh lime, ½ ounce of Demerara syrup, ½ ounce of Raspberry liqueur, and mint leaves. Thankfully, I had mint leaves at home. I use them quite often since they are perfect for tea. I also have lime at home; I use lime zest to make cilantro and jasmine rice. I am glad I can get all the ingredients from the package store. This way, I won't have to go to another store. After purchasing what I needed for my pity party, I returned home.

Once I got in the house, I placed a food delivery order. It seemed like a good evening for Chinese food. There is nothing like House Fried Rice and a Vegetable Spring Roll to end a stressful day. Knowing that delivering my food would take about twenty to thirty minutes, I jumped in the shower to start my evening. How in the world can I decompress after one of the worst days of my life? This particular situation caused my heart to drop and my stomach to bubble. I know with God, this too shall pass. I know that it will pass because He has brought me out before, and remembering what God has done for me in the past is a reminder that - Psalm 30:5 - *weeping may endure for a night but joy comes in the morning.*

I knew my marriage was coming to an end, but to receive the divorce papers from my husband, or should I say, my soon-to-be ex-husband, who moved out with no warning or discussion, I was surprised and beyond feeling betrayed. I gave Reggie twenty-five years, one-quarter of a century, two and a half decades, and most troubling, almost half of my life. I am fifty-two years old with three children. One graduated from college and resides on his own. One is currently in college. The youngest, the only girl, and the most spoiled of the bunch is my fourteen-year-old daughter. Yes, my husband left the baby girl behind, whom he claims to love so much.

Although the past few years were tumultuous in the house, most dissension was between my husband and the kids. However, the brunt of his unhappiness was taken out on me. My husband did not like me taking up for the children. He had the impression that I was going against him. I was doing what most mothers would do.

I was trying to keep the peace, especially since confrontation is not my strong suit.

After receiving the divorce papers, I cried and cried uncontrollably. Reggie would not discuss what I should expect. I would call him, and my calls would go to voicemail. I would text him, and my text messages were unanswered. Remember that we still had a teenage daughter, Cai, at home. After everything Reggie put us through, I should not have been surprised that the kids were excited to see him leave. Although I was crying, the kids were ready to throw a party because he was gone. He left on the 13th of August. This was the weekend my son, daughter, and I took our middle child back to college. This particular weekend was Reggie's mother's 70th birthday party. Not to anyone's surprise, Reggie attended her party instead of accompanying us as we took Doug back to school to start his second year of college.

No one knew, but Doug was a high-functioning autistic young man. Back then, it was called Asperger's Syndrome, which has now merged with other disorders into the autism spectrum disorder. This syndrome causes social and communication difficulties. Having Autism, Doug keeps to himself the majority of the time. He interacts with others when necessary. He is a gamer and takes great pride in coding, creating emulators, and developing games. Doug is also a phenomenal artist.

I felt so bad for the children because they once again had to be subjected to their dad's incomprehensible behavior. It was like watching a two-year-old throw a temper tantrum. Instead of keeping his foolishness in the house, he decided to take it outside this time. We went to get something to eat before getting on the road. Reggie got home and thought he missed saying goodbye to Doug. Not knowing we were only ten minutes away from the house and having to blame someone for his irresponsible actions, he took it out on Al, throwing all his belongings into the yard because he thought Al was why we left since he was driving to NC. Reggie had thrown out the dog cage, clothes, shoes, and Al's computer and monitor he needed for his job. We pulled up to the house so that Reggie could tell Doug goodbye, and when I saw all of Al's belongings in the yard, I knew this would not end well. Reggie was unaware that we were getting food before we hit the road. We figured we would eat while we waited for him to get home. Reggie came flying out of the house, cursing and screaming at all of us. I had the kids pick up Al's things off the lawn and place them in the van. Reggie was outside, acting like the Tasmanian Devil. I asked him if he was crazy and why he threw all of Al's items on the front lawn. Reggie said he did it because we could not wait five to ten minutes for him to return and tell Doug goodbye. Well, Reggie told us he would be home in ten minutes. Those ten minutes turned into an hour before we decided to get something to eat. Needless to say, communication was non-existent that day.

Reggie left at 9 am that morning, and this confrontation occurred at 4:00 pm. He wanted us to wait for him to stop running the streets to tell his son goodbye. Then he said he was worth our waiting for. I internally disputed that comment. The way he was acting, I dare not say anything out loud.

Cai was so scared that she called the police. The 9-1-1 operator asked Cai to stay on the phone with her until the police arrived; we were still waiting an hour later. During this time, Reggie was in Al's face, making intimidating gestures and screaming at the top of his lungs. If ever I thought I saw the devil in action, this was the time. I could see the fear and terror in Al's face. As Cai and Doug walked around the side of the house towards Reggie, he squared up as if he were going to hit them. I asked Reggie to calm down. Unbeknownst to me, Al had called Reggie's mother to tell her what was happening. At that time, she told Al that Reggie didn't need to be there with his PTSD. No one had any idea that Reggie was diagnosed with PTSD. Was that something his mother made up to condone Reggie's behavior? Nonetheless, she told Al she was on her way. When the police and Reggie's mother arrived, we were already on the highway—I-285 East to 85 North.

The kids decided that dealing with their dad and his mother was enough. The kids cut off all communication with both of them. Interestingly, the children had seen their grandmother's antics before this confrontation. Still, they tried to love and respect her regardless because she was "grandma." They now refer to her as the toxic influencer. Grandmothers are supposed to be loving and caring. The rest of her family let her do and say what she wanted, but that got old after a while for me. Her controlling spirit was enough for me to keep her at arm's length. The kid's grandmother was loving and caring until you turned your back; then, she was there with a knife – waiting to stab you in the back with it. She would advise Reggie, thinking she was instructing him how a mother should. She did not realize he was lying to her. She would encourage him - based on a lie, and now both were walking around looking and sounding foolish, especially to people who knew the truth.

Before the pandemic, Reggie's mother would always convey how lonely she was and how she was so depressed. At the start of the pandemic, Reggie went to his mother's house to work from there instead of staying at home with his family. I thought this would be an opportunity to allow our family to grow closer, not become more disconnected. I did not believe he worked from there

Monday through Friday while the kids and I were home until she told us how happy she was that he would come to her house every day to work. She said that she is no longer alone with him there all the time. She was correct. She was no longer lonely; however, his kids were. They wanted their father home. Cai started noticing she was no longer his priority; his mother was, which left Cai hurt and depressed. Reggie's mother did not seem to care what she was doing to our family as long as things went her way.

Ana always portrayed herself as the nicest, most stand-up Christian; once the veil was removed, you would see the true her. I am glad I know God for myself because if I had to base becoming a Christian on her words and actions, I would prefer to stay in the streets instead of the church. As much as she reads her bible, I think she purposely missed Genesis 2:24 – *Therefore shall a man leave his father and mother, and shall cleave unto his wife: and they shall be one flesh.*

CHAPTER 1

What Was I Thinking?

My oldest son, Al, is a product of my first marriage. My first husband and I should have never gotten married. Apparently, my second husband and I should not have gotten married either. Nonetheless, although my first husband and I were adults, we were too immature to have a real adult relationship. I had been in Atlanta for a few months before I met him. I went to Bowlero Marietta, a bowling alley on Delk Rd. in Marietta, Ga. I have always been a gamer, so I was excited when I saw there were arcade games. I have a magnet connected to me when I enter any arcade; I am always immediately drawn to Galaga.

I was not looking for a relationship, but when I looked at who played the video game next to me, I had to rethink that. This man stood about 6'2, had pecan brown skin color, and had his hair and beard lined. He was fine. I guess he was checking me out, too, because when he finished his game, he stood next to my game and said, you are pretty good at this. KA-BOOM, I lost that battleship. He said I am sorry. I did not mean to distract you. KA-BOOM, I lost a second battleship. He started laughing.

Usually, I don't lose that quickly, but I was a little nervous with this fine man beside me. Are you here with anyone? I said yes. He apologized, saying he did not mean to be disrespectful. He turned around to walk away. All I could think was that he was fine and respectful - a perfect combination. Before I missed my opportunity, I quickly said, I am here with my cousins. Are you here with anyone, I asked. He said; I am here with my cousin and his girlfriend. He asked me to sit down with him for a minute. I followed him to the table where his cousin was. He went to introduce me but did not know my name. I held my hand out to shake his cousin's hand. Hi, I am Parris. His cousin's girlfriend quickly jumped up, held her hand out, and said hi, I am Stacey. I shook her hand and said hello. I guess she wanted me to know her man was off-limits.

My cousins were bowling about three lanes over. One of my cousins came to find me and said, hey, Parris, it's your turn. We can skip you if you want. Yes, please let the next person bowl. I will be there soon. I introduced my new friend to my cousin. This is um... my friend interrupted me, realizing we had not exchanged names; he held his hand out, shook my cousin's hand, and said, "My name is Eddie. Not familiar with my new friend, my cousin shook Eddie's hand while looking in my direction, perplexed. I advised my cousin to skip me, and I would be right over. Eddie and I exchanged phone numbers. I did not want to be rude, so I joined my cousins to finish the night with them. After about another forty-five minutes, Eddie was getting ready to leave. He came to our lane, hugged me, and told me to use the card he gave me. I am 5'8, and Eddie is 6 inches taller than me; I had to reach up to hug him. I looked up at him and noticed he had some of the biggest, prettiest eyes and a bright smile. All teeth are present and accounted for. This man was fine!

CHAPTER 2

An Affair? You Got to Go!

After a couple of years of on-and-off dating, we went to the courthouse and tied the knot. Our marriage did not last long, but I at least got my oldest son – Al, out of it. Eddie was so excited when Al was born. Eddie's mother came down from Indiana for a few days and helped me when I returned from the hospital. Al was her first grandchild, and she spoiled him rotten. My parents came down from D.C. after Eddie's mother left so they could help me. I was so happy to have help. I had no idea what I was doing. My sister had two children, but she had them after I moved to Georgia, so I had no experience with a baby.

About a year after Al was born, I found out Eddie was having an affair. After I found out, I packed his clothes in a black trash bag with a note saying Trina said to bring this bag to her house. I put the trash bag outside the door. Yes, he had keys to the apartment, but at that point, he knew he better not step foot in the apartment we used to share. I was so befuddled by this girl's actions. She had the audacity to call me and tell me she had been seeing my husband. She introduced herself to me when she called.

Hi, my name is Trina. I gave Eddie a deadline to let you know we have been seeing each other. He said you would not understand and would be hurt. I don't think it's fair for you not to know your husband and I are in love and we plan on being together. I asked her if she was serious and how she got my number. She hesitated to answer any of my questions.

I told her to get off my phone and never, not ever, to call me again. I don't know why I waited for her to hang up first. She said, please listen. I saw Eddie at my friend's house during a party, and he was tall and handsome. We were attracted to each other. You were attracted to a married man, I asked. I didn't know he was married immediately. I am not the kind of person who would have an affair, but it was something about him I could not resist. Even when I found out he was married, I should not have been, but I was okay with it. I guess that is what I will tell our baby when he is old enough to ask why his daddy does not live with us. She yelled, BABY?!?! He did not tell me he had a baby! Well, now you know. That's when I hung up on TT.

I did not want to hear any more of what she was saying. About an hour after being slapped in the face with this information, Eddie tried to call me to test the waters. He was trying to find out if he could ease his way back home. Why don't you check with TT to find out what we discussed? He asked who is TT? I told him Trifling Trina. Please tell her not to call me anymore. I told Eddie I would make this easy for him. I will file for divorce. Just let me know what address to send the divorce papers to. Eddie had the nerve to ask me what I was talking about. Before I hung up on him, I assured him I would not keep him away from his son.

CHAPTER 3

The Wrong Man

Men and women should be responsible for being in their child's life. There is no reason for a child to grow up not knowing who their parents are. I told him we would make arrangements for him to see his son. Since Eddie was a cook at a restaurant and his schedule fluctuated weekly, we kept a copy of the schedule on the refrigerator so that I could keep up with his work hours and off days. I asked him to complete the schedule for the upcoming week and provide me a copy weekly to know when I can expect him to visit his son. He asked me why I needed to know when he would come by. Are you seriously asking me why I need to know when you are coming over? Does it matter? I am asking you to inform me out of respect for my time and privacy. He asked me if it was because I was seeing someone. I could do nothing but laugh. It's not like I owe you an answer, but I want to ensure Al is ready if you want to take him out. I will speak with an attorney and get divorce proceedings started so that you and your girlfriend can enjoy each other's company without any strings attached to me other than our baby. This way, you will have the freedom you seem to want.

Six months later, I accepted a job in Virginia. I did not want to move, but raising a child as a single parent, I knew I needed to be closer to my family since Al's donor decided he did not have time to help with his son. Eddie was not happy when I told him I was moving. After multiple nights of Eddie showing up after Al was in bed and asleep, I was excited to move. I asked him what baby was awake between 11 pm and 2 am for parental visitation. I was tired of this buffoonery. Eddie would stand outside the apartment door, banging on the door and calling my name until I opened the door. I was tired of the complaints from the neighbors. One neighbor called the police because she thought he was trying to break in. Knowing that Virginia was at least an eight-hour drive, I knew I would get some peace, and Al and I would be able to start our lives over.

A year after the final divorce, Al's father and girlfriend welcomed a baby girl. I sent them a congratulations card. Putting my pride aside was difficult, but Al now had a sister with whom I would want him to have a relationship. All babies are a blessing regardless of their parents or how they came to exist.

We moved into Lee Overlook Apartments in Centerville, VA. Our apartment overlooked the creek that ran behind the flats. It was so lovely and serene. Al kept running between the bedrooms, the living room, and the kitchen. He was so excited. I cannot lie; so was I. I had three days before I started the new position. Thankfully, the moving company would be delivering our belongings soon.

CHAPTER 4

A **New Start in A New Land**

Only four of us were in the training class on my first day in the new position. The trainer must have had at least two cups of coffee before she started. She was full of energy. A lot more energy than any of us had put together. I felt like a child attending a new school on the first day. I knew no one in this class. However, there was one lady I immediately felt a connection with. She carried the disposition of my grandmother, was straightforward, and had a tremendous amount of class.

After our training class, it was time to start Tier I Technical Support. I was somewhat nervous since I was a bit unsure of my duties. There was a network engineer, Reggie, with whom we tried to avoid working. Because of all the trouble tickets, the network engineer returned for follow-up; we labeled him the I-I King. I-I is a trouble ticket status considered incomplete or incorrect if any missing information hinders the technician from working on the trouble ticket. If the ticket were not perfect, this engineer would send the ticket back so we could correct the issue before working on any part of the ticket. Interestingly, he was the only engineer with whom we would have this problem constantly.

The number of tickets Reggie kept returning to me made me feel he was indirectly telling me that I was not doing my job to his satisfaction. I realized this was an opportunity to learn. With every ticket he would send back, I would ask him to call me and explain what was incomplete or incorrect. As he saw that I was interested in learning, he would call me to show me what I missed and educate me on what some of my peers did incorrectly.

The more we talked, the more interested we became in each other. Reggie was so insightful regarding technology, 401Ks, and different types of retirements. I was initially not interested in any retirement information, but Reggie took the time to give me advice that would benefit my son and me. I was only interested in a technical position once I met Reggie. He encouraged me to look into what was next for my career. I started researching the requirements for technical job postings in Atlanta, GA.

Even though I did not expect to get a call for an interview for one of the technical positions I saw in the job postings, I applied anyway. I received a call from HR requesting to set up an interview. I was so excited yet anxious. Nightly, Reggie and I would have mock interviews until the interview. After weeks of this, I felt comfortable with my comprehension of the subject matter and looked forward to the interview.

The interview lasted approximately thirty minutes. I thought it was a great interview. Although the interviewer told me I would hear something within the next seven days, weeks passed, and I did not hear anything. I assumed that meant I did not get the position.

CHAPTER 5

She Tried to Get Me Fired

My director approached my desk and asked if I would come to his office. Not having any idea what this was regarding, I assumed it had to do with the job I applied for. He told me that he received a call from a young lady who accused me of calling her job and harassing her. He also told me she said the phone company traced the call to my desk phone. Denying this, I assured him that I would never do that. He said the young lady would not give her name. I could not think of anyone who had any animosity against me other than Trina. Although Al and I moved out of Georgia, she still seemed threatened by my very existence. I kept trying to figure out why. She had her man, and they had a new baby. Why would she not leave me alone? When confronted with this foolishness, I informed my director that I had just gone through a divorce and moved to Virginia to get away from my ex-husband and his girlfriend. Knowing my company was on my side and I had nothing to worry about, I felt more at ease. I was advised that the voice group would be checking the switches and attempting to trace the call to find out where she was calling from. My director told me he knew the individual was being deceptive.

He said if I had called from my desk phone, there would be no way for the phone company to trace a call back to my desk. They would only be able to trace the call back to the PBX. I had no idea what all of that meant. I told the young lady I would talk to you regarding her accusations and asked her to call back to follow up. I do not anticipate she will call back, but if she does, I will let her know that the harassment is coming from her, and if it happens again, I will be filing charges on behalf of the company against her. Thank you so much for letting me know what is going on. My director looked me in my eyes and reassured me I had nothing to worry about. He suggested I take the rest of the day off. I let my director know I would be okay to finish my shift, but he insisted I take off the rest of the day. I packed up and left. I went outside, took a deep breath, and went home. I did not go to pick up Al from the babysitter's house for a couple of hours. I went to a park and just sat around thinking about what was next in my life.

The next day came so quickly. As I walked into the building, it felt like all eyes were on me. I wondered if my director, Art, told my peers what I was dealing with. The closer I got to my desk, the better I felt.

CHAPTER 6

A **True Friend Only Loves - Never Judges**

Gi-Gi approached me, put her hand on my shoulder, and asked if I was okay. After ensuring Gi-Gi I was all right and needed a little time off, she told me she would like to have my home phone number before we left for the day. Tears started welling up in my eyes, and she asked me to come with her to the break room. I did not go into detail because I did not want to start crying out of control – again. Gi-Gi told me she and her husband were there whenever I needed them. Gi-Gi is one of the most elegant women I have ever met, handling herself with great dignity and poise.

Gi-Gi lived a few blocks from the job and has become one of the best friends I could ever ask for. She is like having an auntie, a mother, a sister, and a friend all in one. You can get the kind of advice that makes sense. She will not sugarcoat anything. She would pray that your heart is prepared to receive worlds of wisdom and then would tell you the truth about any situation. She is a fantastic friend and a marvelous blessing. After being in the training class with her, I knew God had put her and her husband in my life. They assured me they would be there to help if I needed anything. Some people use this phrase as a cliche. However, she and her husband mean it. I love these two tremendously.

Gi-Gi and her husband, Kent, had the most beautiful African artwork and wooden African statues. Al loved going to their place until he saw the statues. He would start crying, but he kept looking. I assured him that if he stopped looking, he would be okay. He would do the same at Sweetwater Tavern, a restaurant with fantastic food and scenery. The restaurant had lights that hung down with cowboys on metal horses. These horses and cowboys were at most six inches in height. Al would look at the lights and start crying. It was not just a small cry but a cry that required him to take a deep breath and then scream. Thankfully, the waitress got us some paper and crayons to draw Al's attention away from the scenery. Al's calm only lasted for about fifteen minutes. He would look at the lights again, and the cycle started over. I began to question the intelligence of my baby. Of course, any of Al's lack of intelligence was from his father's DNA.

CHAPTER 7

ove Has No Place For Insecurity

After about one or two years of living in Virginia, I was ready to make another move. I was interested in moving from a Tier I technical help desk position to a Tier II engineer position. I wanted to fix the trouble instead of just opening tickets on the problem.

After a few months of talking off of the clock, it was time for Reggie and I to meet in person. I had a training class in Atlanta, GA. The training was unrelated to the position I applied for. For the past few months, we engaged in conversation sight unseen. So, yes, I was extremely nervous. Would I be attractive enough? Would I be what he was looking for? Would I dress the way he wanted? Would he be embarrassed to be seen with me? My insecurities were at an all-time high. The thoughts went on and on and on.

He asked me to stay with him. Of course, I was reluctant. He said I promise we will have a good time. I chuckled because I started recollecting episodes of women missing on Unsolved Mysteries. Since I work evenings, you will be at my place while I am at work. By the time I get off and get home, it will be time for you to get up and go to the training class. He lived down the street from the location of the training. Al stayed with my cousins – Al's godparents. Of course, Al's godparents wanted to know all there was to know about Reggie. Where did he live? Where did he work?

His home and work phone? I am surprised they did not ask for his social security number and mother's maiden name. Although I knew we were a little more than friends, I assured my cousins we were just friends.

Reggie took off from work on the last day of my training. He picked me up in his black Honda Prelude. We went to the movies and saw "Life" starring Eddie Murphy, Bernie Mac, Martin Lawrence, and Obba Babatunde. After watching the film, we went to eat at Applebee's Bar and Grille. It was the one located on Franklin Rd. in Marietta, GA. Reggie asked if I wanted to do anything while I was in Georgia since I had two more days before it was time for Al and me to return to Virginia. After we ate, we sat and talked for at least another hour.

Time went so quickly. It was like talking to an old friend. We went back to Reggie's apartment. He was such a gentleman. He opened the car door for me. I had no idea men still did that. I am not sure why chivalry is dead. Men would get so much more love, compassion, attention, and almost anything else – *almost anything* - if they would resurrect chivalry. I cannot fathom the vast majority of women say they don't need a man to open doors or hold doors open for them. Reggie stayed in Post Village Apartments off Cobb Parkway. Of course, I wondered what his salary was - a nice car, a beautifully furnished apartment, and a fashionable selection of clothes.

Reggie and I were enjoying one another. I enjoyed how Reggie treated me like I was the only woman in the world. I wish time would slow down. After returning to his apartment, we sat on his sofa, watched TV, and talked. He was such a good communicator. He listened while I spoke. He put his arm around my shoulder, and I just melted. He knew that because he moved closer to me and held me tighter. He kissed me and asked if I wanted anything to drink. I said yes, even though I didn't want anything. I was just nervous and needed something to do with my hands. So, holding a glass was perfect.

CHAPTER 8

Making Room In My Heart For Love
Reggie slept on his sofa, and I slept in his bed. I woke up to the smell of bacon. I went to the restroom, cleaned my face, and brushed my teeth. I sat at the table, and he had bacon, pancakes, eggs, and potatoes on the table. A carafe of orange juice, a bottle of champagne, and two tall, slender champagne flutes on the table. Mimosas? I asked. Are you trying to get me drunk early in the morning? Nope, I want to toast to the best weekend I have had in what feels like an eternity. I got up, walked over to him, and kissed him. After eating, I asked him what he had planned for the day. He said I was getting ready to ask you the same thing. He said he thought about a movie and relaxing. I was fine going to the movies and then returning to relax since it was raining. After we cleaned up from breakfast, I showered and dressed. He said I thought we were staying in today. I told him I thought we were going to the movies and then coming back to rest. He said he ordered a movie from an online service; that way, we can stay in and relax. He had spoken with my cousins to ensure they were okay watching Al while we hung out. Reggie had me totally and completely enamored with him. He was too good to be true.

I returned to his room, changed out of my going-out clothes, and put on comfy clothes. I put on a T-shirt and a pair of shorts. I was so excited to sit here with Reggie. We discussed what I learned in the training class. After talking, I asked what movie he had ordered from the online store. "There's Something About Mary." He asked if that movie was okay with me. I had never heard of the movie, but it didn't matter what it was; I was just enjoying spending time with him. I grabbed the throw cover from the back of the sofa and put it over my legs. Reggie pulled up the online movie service and started "There's Something About Mary." He got under the throw cover with me. Once again, butterflies started in my stomach. To be this close to him made me feel so secure.

The movie There's Something About Mary stars Cameron Diaz, Matt Dillon, and Ben Stiller. I don't care how good the movie is; I will fall asleep. The part of the movie I saw was hilarious. I woke up with my head on Reggie's shoulder, and his arm was around me. He said I only missed about fifteen minutes of the movie. I looked up at him and apologized for falling asleep. He said he did not mind and let me know that my falling asleep on him meant I was comfortable with him.

CHAPTER 9

Who Is Your Number One, Me or Her?
We were looking into each other's eyes when the phone rang. Reggie let his answering machine pick up - "Hello, Reginald. I have not heard from you this weekend. Are you okay? I thought you were going to come over today." I pretended I didn't hear the message. When I moved over a little from Reggie, he chuckled. With much attitude, I asked, what is funny? He asked if I could move back closer to him. I didn't know you had someplace to go. I don't want to stop you. He grinned and said give me a minute. I thought to myself, no, this negro is not getting ready to return a phone call. Hey momma. I am fine.

Don't you remember Parris coming down from Virginia for training? We are sitting around watching movies and talking. Reggie laughed, handing me the phone. I tried to push the phone away, but he insistently pushed the phone towards me. I rolled my eyes, took the phone, and said, hello.

After Reggie's mother asked how I was doing, I reciprocated the question, asking how she was feeling. She said I am doing fair to middling. I thought to myself, what is a fair to middling? She asked about my training and if Reggie and I were enjoying ourselves. Yes, Reggie and I are having a wonderful time. After a few more minutes of small talk, I asked if she would like to speak back to him. She said yes. I told her it was nice talking to her and hoped to meet her soon. She said it was nice speaking to you too - I love you. My mouth was open, thinking, should I reciprocate the words, I love you? This moment was awkward, mainly since my mother and I exchanged I love you so infrequently. It's not that I don't love my mother; it's just that we did not say "I love you" often. I said, aw, thank you. I am grateful. That means a lot to me. I returned the phone to Reggie. He said, okay, momma, I will talk to you later. We are going to stay inside today since it is raining out.

I was so embarrassed that I tried to divert the conversation because I knew what he was going to say. So, Reggie, do you want to go out for dinner? He said, don't think you will get out of discussing that phone call or, better yet, what transpired before the phone call. I asked him what he expected me to do - did you expect me to hear a female leave you a message about not hearing from you or seeing you and think I would not have any questions? He said, why didn't you ask me questions instead of getting upset? What was I supposed to say? Who is this woman leaving you messages? Reggie responded; Yes, that is exactly what you should have asked! I told him we had not established a relationship that gives me the right to question what you are doing or who you are doing it with. He said jokingly, we have established a relationship – I fixed you breakfast and took you out to dinner. I had to laugh. He moved closer to me and held me in his arms. He said although we have not discussed exclusively seeing one another, I want nothing more than to take our relationship to the next level. Again, my stomach is doing flip-flops. I was so ecstatic. I was falling for Reggie. We looked into each other's eyes and kissed.

So, back to my original question: do you want to eat out for dinner? He said, no – I want to make you dinner. Do we need to go to the store? Nope, I went shopping yesterday; I am all prepared to cook. Reggie, I can get used to this. He told me to relax on the sofa while he started dinner. I couldn't let him cook alone, so I decided to help. I hand-washed, rinsed, dried, and put away the dishes as he cooked. By the time Reggie finished cooking dinner, the kitchen was spotless. My mouth was watering. We both had a glass of wine and a salad, then fried Swai, fried bay scallops, and potatoes. After dinner, we enjoyed a bowl of cherry sorbet. A good movie, good food, and an exceptional man, how could I ask for any more?

CHAPTER 10

Hanging Out with My Babies
After eating, I called Al, who was still with his godparents. I let Al stay with them because I was not ready for him to spend an extensive amount of time with someone I was not well-acquainted with. When Al got on the phone, surprisingly, he did not want to speak to me; he tried to talk to Reggie. I was utterly shocked. I looked at Reggie with a surprising look on my face. Reggie asked, what was wrong? I told him the phone was for him. Reggie engaged him in conversation as if they were old friends. I could not be happier.

I only had one day left to be with the man who captured my heart. I did not want to go back to Virginia yet. One thing Reggie found out was that I am not a drinker. Yes, I had one glass of wine and was extremely sleepy. We lay down talking, and the next thing I knew, I was waking up looking around a dark room, trying to figure out where I was. Nothing in this room looked familiar. I looked next to me, and Reggie was asleep. I laughed internally, not believing I had fallen asleep talking to him. He probably thinks I am so rude. It was about 4 am, and I was completely awake. I went into the living room and reviewed my training class notes. I could not focus because all I could think about was how amazing the past few days had been. I pulled the throw cover over my legs again and just curled up. I turned the television on and turned it down very low, trying not to wake Reggie. I guess I fell asleep again because now Reggie was waking me up. Reggie leaned down and asked me if I wanted to go out and get something to eat. It was 8 am, and Reggie was already dressed and ready to go out. I guess it was my turn to get ready.

After showering and getting dressed, I needed to check on Al. I missed my baby. I called my cousin, and they had already gone out for breakfast. I told them I would get Al after we got a bite to eat. We went to Cracker Barrel on Delk Rd. in Marietta. I had never been to Cracker Barrel. Not even when I previously lived in Georgia. It was interesting; walking into the restaurant, you walk through the store full of nostalgic candies and toys. Once the host seated us, I let Reggie order for me. We both had the same thing – Grandpa's Country Fried Breakfast. Two scrambled eggs with cheese, Country Fried Chicken with Sawmill Gravy, and Loaded Hashbrown Casserole. Reggie and I talked over breakfast. I cannot believe how we meshed. It was like hanging out with an old friend. We briefly talked about our families. After not seeing any pictures of his family at his apartment, I decided it might be better to discuss what I learned in the training class instead of learning about each of our families.

Reggie paid the bill after we ate. We were forty-five minutes from Alpharetta, GA, a prosperous city north of Atlanta where Al's Godparents lived. We pulled up to their house, and Al came running outside. Mommy – Reggie. Why did you leave me so long? I told him I had training classes for work. Al stated that sure was a lot of training as he walked away from me. Al disappeared into the house and started walking back out with his suitcase. As if I needed permission from a two-year-old, I asked Al if I could talk to Aunt Robin and Uncle Dan before we left. Okay, mommy, but it's time to go. Robin asked if we had any plans for the rest of the day. I looked at Reggie because I had not thought about asking him that. Reggie said; I have a surprise for Parris and the little fellow. I glanced at Reggie and told him I don't do well with surprises, so if it involves meeting anyone, please let me know beforehand. He said, no, it does not include meeting anyone; you are safe.

CHAPTER 11

Blended Families Can Be Created from Love

Reggie was taking the car seat out of Robin's car and putting it in his car. Watching Reggie attempt to put a car seat in a Honda Prelude Sports Car was comical. After checking to ensure it was secure, I thanked Al's Godparents and hugged them before we pulled out and headed to our surprise. By this time, it was 2 pm. So, where is my surprise? You will see.

I went to ask Al if he was excited and find out how he enjoyed himself; however, Al was already asleep. Well, I guess he had a good time. Reggie pulled up to a Christmas Tree lot. We woke Al up and walked around the lot until we found a small but full tree. The tree was no taller than 6 feet. Reggie must have been ready for this because he got a car cover out of his trunk and draped it over the roof of his car so that the

tree would not scratch the paint. We went back to Reggie's apartment and put the Christmas Tree up. He had purchased the tree stand and all of the decorations already. Al was so excited to see the decorations and the lights come to life. Al was jumping up and down and yelling turn on the lights, turn on the lights. It was just about dusk, so we should be able to see the tree light up. It was beautiful. Reggie stood back and looked at the tree for a few seconds. Are you okay, I asked. Yes, I just have not done this in years. Well, you did a great job. He moved towards Al and me, put his arm around me, and said, no, we did a great job, and then he kissed me on the cheek and picked up Al.

Okay, it's time for the second surprise. Second surprise? The Christmas tree was not the surprise? Nope, the Christmas tree was Al's surprise. I hugged Reggie and gave him a peck on the lips. We got ready to go back out. We stopped at Sonic Drive-In. Reggie pulled into one of the bays and ordered. Al was happy to get a hot dog and some tots. Reggie and I split a Footlong Quarter Pound Coney with chili. We sat there eating and listening to Christmas songs for another thirty to forty-five minutes. By this time, it was dark, and we were heading to Garden Lights, Holiday Nights at Atlanta's Botanical Garden.

Al fell asleep again in the car. He woke to an array of Christmas lights. Al went from groggy to beyond excited. He started kicking his legs, which resulted in him kicking Reggie's seat. I turned around to tell Al to stop, and Reggie put his hand on my knee and told me Al was excited and it was okay. Reggie hurried to get Al out of his car seat before walking around to open my door. As we admired the Christmas lights, I held Al's hand, and Reggie held Al's other hand. We received quite a few compliments about being such a beautiful family. Reggie and I looked at each other, smiled, and said thank you. Neither of us corrected anyone. We just basked in the compliments. After walking around for a while, Al started to get tired. Reggie picked Al up and put him on his neck while we returned to the car. Reggie took my hand in his, and I wanted to melt.

CHAPTER 12

L eaving Is So Hard to Do

Reggie put Al in his car seat, and after I checked the seat belt, Reggie kissed me before he opened my car door. Even though we had been getting to know each other over the past 6-8 months over the phone, there was something about being in his arms. We rode back to Reggie's place pretty much in silence. I was unsure what that meant. I mean, we have been talking since I got there. When we returned to Reggie's, Al was asleep, so Reggie and I sat in the car for a few minutes before I asked him if he was okay. He said the past few days were perfect and some of the best days of his life. I do not want you and Al to go back to Virginia. I reassured him that he could always come and visit us in Virginia, or we could always come back to Georgia. That's when Reggie surprised me; he said that whether Al and I moved to Georgia or whether he moved to Virginia, he did not want a long-distance relationship. I asked if we were in a relationship. He looked at me, confused. I chuckled, smiled, leaned in, and kissed him. I told him I was kidding. We already established earlier that we were in a relationship. That's when Reggie's face softened.

After another hour of conversing in the car, he got Al out of his car seat and carried him into his apartment. When I got into the apartment, I started to pack our suitcase since our flight left early in the morning. As I packed my clothes, tears started rolling down my cheek. I tried to hurry up and wipe the tears away before Reggie could see them. That was unsuccessful. Although my skin tone is caramel brown, my cheeks and nose turn rosy red when I laugh or cry. Reggie knew I had not been laughing, so the only other option was crying.

A few more tears fell as Reggie came in and held me in his arms. When Reggie asked me what was wrong, I told him I am not usually this emotional. I told him I was not ready to leave him. Being with him made me feel like I found the one God intended for me to share the rest of my life with. I continued to pack, and Reggie got ready for bed. When Reggie got out of the shower and prepared for bed, my bags were at the front door. By the time I got out of the shower, Reggie was sitting on the sofa watching ESPN. Reggie had already put Al in his bed and told me I could sleep with Al and he would stay on the couch.

I sat on the sofa with Reggie, and we talked about a lot. I learned more about him being in the military, which was comical and exciting. He even showed me some of his military pictures. We sat in silence for a few more minutes, and I told him I was going to go to bed since we had a long day ahead of us. He agreed and kissed me; good night.

I was more tired than I thought. I laid down next to Al, and the next thing I knew, the alarm clock was going off. I tried to turn the alarm off before Al woke up. I like to let him sleep as long as possible. I turned over, and Al was not in bed. As I put my legs over the side of the bed to get this day started, there was a smell that was so familiar: ah, bacon and toast. Well, good morning I said, smiling. What a pleasant surprise. Mommy, Mommy, look what me and Reggie did – look at what Reggie and I did, I said, correcting his grammar. Yup, look what we did. I felt hopeless trying to correct him again; he was too excited. Wow, you fixed me breakfast. Yup. After I got out of the bathtub. You already took a bath? He said, yup, let me finish my story. After I got out of the bathtub, we cooked you breakfast. I put butter on the toast. I spilled a little bit of juice, but Reggie wiped it up.

Reggie said, I knew you were tired, so Al and I went to the store to get some bath-wash. He picked out the kind he said you have at home. I greatly appreciate you taking care of Al and allowing me to rest. I wanted to avoid causing you any extra trouble. I apologize. I forgot about getting his bath-wash from his godparents. I sat at the table and thanked Reggie and Al for fixing breakfast. We held hands, and Reggie said grace. I made a sandwich from my toast and bacon since I knew we did not have much time before we had to go.

Did I find myself a praying, cooking, compassionate, and loving man? I did not feel like I was compromising any of my beliefs or my desires. II Corinthians 6:14 *Be ye not unequally yoked together with unbelievers: for what fellowship hath righteousness with unrighteousness? and what communion hath light with darkness?* As Reggie started praying, "Thank You, Lord God, Al mocked him in his cute baby voice.

CHAPTER 13

Airport Drama

After we finished breakfast, we headed to the airport. It was a thirty-minute ride from Reggie's apartment to Hartsfield-Jackson Airport. I still do not understand how Atlanta has what seems like a twenty-four-hour rush hour. We finally made it to the airport in one piece. The Atlanta police ensured you pulled to the curb, got out, got your bags, and went on your merry way. There was absolutely no parking or standing. They did not bother us too much when they saw Reggie getting Al out of the back seat. Our goodbye kiss lasted longer than permitted. Officer Friendly took great pride in blowing his whistle and yelling at us to move along – No Standing, the officer shouted. Reggie gave me one small peck and hugged Al. Al started to cry because he didn't want Reggie to leave. He thought Reggie was coming with us. The signal for the cell phone was not good at the airport; otherwise, I would have called Reggie immediately. Five minutes into the airport, I am already missing Reggie. While Al and I waited to board, Al fell asleep. Al sleeping gave me some quiet time – an opportunity to reflect on the last four days.

I didn't see any pictures of his family, nor did we discuss either of our families in detail. Were we so smitten with one another that we did not discuss anything outside of each other? I didn't know what to expect when I first got to Atlanta. I had no idea this trip would be so pleasant and peaceful.

It is almost time for us to board, and Al is still asleep. I wish we could teleport to our seats so he could stay asleep, but since that was impossible, I woke Al up. Who did I see walking towards us on the way to stand in line to get on the plane? His biological father – Eddie. He walked up to us with his girlfriend on his arm. I wanted them both to be like Samantha on Bewitched – wiggle their nose and disappear. He leaned down to hug Al, and Al screamed, "Leave me alone!" The look on Eddie's face was priceless.

I guess Eddie thought absence made Al's heart grow fonder. In actuality, it made Al forget about him. According to Al's father, I was to blame for this. He said I turned Al against him. I told him he would have to know you to be turned against you. Eddie's girlfriend walked away when Al yelled. After walking away, his girlfriend refused to look in our direction. As we moved closer to the gate, a security guard approached us. The security guard asked if I was okay. I told him yes. Two more security guards showed up. Now, I was embarrassed. Four days of fun ended with this idiot caught up in his feelings. I surmise my four days in heaven was the calm before the storm. Thank God it was time for Al and I to go to our seats. Hopefully, there will be no more drama for the next hour and forty-five minutes. Thankfully, Al went to sleep as soon as the plane took off. I looked out the window and reflected on the past few days. Finally, we were almost back. Al said, Mommy, is the plane going down? I said, sweetie, the plane is descending. Say it with me, de-scend-ing.

CHAPTER 14

Love Outweighs Exhaustion

We finally arrived at Dulles Airport. The drive from the airport to the apartment was only about twenty minutes. We got home. I dropped our suitcases at the front door and collapsed on the sofa. Go figure, the good, the bad, and the ugly, all within the past four hours. I had Al go into his room and play while I fixed him lunch. I called Reggie to let him know we made it back. I told him I would fix Al's lunch and call him back after I took a nap. You know I cannot stop thinking about you and Al. I already miss you two. We miss you too.

I told Reggie I had the best week, and I appreciated him hosting me. He said I want you to meet my family the next time you come to Georgia. That sounds like fun, I told Reggie. Are you sure they will be okay with me having been married and having a child already? If they are not, they will have to internally work through what they are uncomfortable with. Mommy, I am hungry. That is not how you ask for something, Al. Mommy, may I please have something to eat? That is better. Reggie, let me get Al something to eat, and I will call you back. We hung up, and I fixed Al a grilled cheese sandwich and some tomato soup. He watched some of his cartoons and fell asleep. I was grateful because I was so exhausted. I ended up falling asleep on the sofa. I woke up to my alarm going off. It was the alarm I set to keep me on track to put Al in the tub and then put him to bed.

Al was still in his bed, sound asleep. I refused to wake him up to put him in the tub. I will have to get up a little earlier than usual because he will need to take a bath, and he will be hungry in the morning since he has slept through dinner. I woke to the alarm going off again. It sounded so distant. I woke up realizing I had slept on the couch last night. Ugh, I do not want to go to work today. I am so tired. I got off the sofa and turned on the shower. I was dragging this morning. I stood under the shower for at least five minutes, attempting to get energy. I am not a coffee drinker, so this warm shower is all I have to invigorate me. I finished up in the shower and started to fix Al some breakfast. He was not in a good mood this morning. He did not want anything I suggested for breakfast. I finally told him; you can have cereal and toast or nothing. He sat at the table and cried until I finished getting dressed for work. I am so glad I have a boy, a T-shirt, a pair of jeans, and tennis shoes, and out the door we go. I dropped Al off at the babysitter's house and told her he was in a mood and refused to eat breakfast. Pointing to the grits she had cooking on the stove; she reassured me he would be okay.

As soon as I got ready to leave, I asked Al for a hug and a kiss, and he said he wanted Reggie. I turned and looked at him in amazement. Reggie has to go to work today. We can call him when we get home this evening. I asked Al for a hug, and he turned away from me. I pulled his arm, kissed him, and tickled him. Finally, Al hugged me, laughing, and said, I love you, Mommy. That made my heart happy. Now, I can get my day started. I love you too, my sweet baby boy.

CHAPTER 15

Mind Your Business
I got to work and started walking into the building when Mi-Mi met me. Are you dating Reggie? Excuse me, I said, confused. Are you dating Reggie? Why would you ask me that? He was engaged to my best friend. She broke it off with him. I don't feel comfortable discussing my personal life with you, especially at work. I felt completely blindsided. So, was Reggie's rebound me? I felt like a complete fool. Why didn't I ask him about any of his previous relationships? Mi-Mi got me out of my internal conversation and said, well, I hope you don't find out the hard way. Reggie is not someone you want to date or even want your son around. It took all I had in my body to hold back the tears. I know until I follow up, I should not listen to what people say, but when I was telling him about my failed marriage, it seemed like he would have taken that opportunity to inform me of his previous engagement.

When I got inside, I immediately went to the restroom and washed my face. I sat down at my desk and took my first call. You never put on a sad face before the enemy; now, Mi-Mi is the enemy. She completely ruined my morning and possibly my relationship. Mi-Mi sat behind me, and I could feel her stares at the back of my head. I opened the first trouble ticket incorrectly. I missed information and saw the ticket come back in my queue. What had

I done incorrectly now? With missing information, I knew what was coming next - a call from the technician. Not five minutes later, I received the call – this is Parris. Hey, Parris, what is going on? Um, not much. How are you? I am doing well, beautiful. As soon as I heard "beautiful," my stomach started with the butterflies again. Most women enjoy receiving compliments. I wanted to turn around, look at Mi-Mi, and stick my tongue out at her. I refrained from being Petty Paula until I knew Reggie's side of the story. We discussed my ticket and what I should have done regarding opening my ticket correctly. We conversed about how much I enjoyed the training class and how well the company took good care of me on my business trip.

I do not think I am not being naïve, but I have thrown out what Mi-Mi said this morning. After picking Al up from the babysitter, I rushed home to call Reggie. Maybe I should not have been so hurried to get home. Two blocks from the apartment, I heard sirens. Being the law-abiding citizen I am, I pulled over to the right to let the police go by. As I looked in the rearview mirror, it was clear I was not as law-abiding as I thought. The police pulled up directly behind me. Al, having a grandfather and a grandmother on the police force, thought it was playtime. He saw the officer's uniform and called out – Granddad. The officer looked at me and looked in the backseat at Al and said, "No, little man, I am not Granddad." I apologize, officer; my parents are both on the police force, so he saw your uniform and immediately thought it was his grandfather. The officer chuckled and told me he could not give me a ticket after being entertained by the little man. He told me to slow down and winked at me. As I rolled the window up, I took a deep breath and thanked the Lord for finding mercy. Al said thank you,

Jesus! Proverbs 22:16 *Train up a child in the way he should go: and when he is old, he will not depart from it.*

CHAPTER 16

Get Out of My Head and Let Me Love

As we got home, I could hear my phone ringing. I tried to hurry up and get into the apartment to answer the phone. I looked at the caller ID and smiled. It was Reggie. I told myself I would call him back after I got Al situated. Thirty minutes after getting in the house, Reggie called again. I made it to the phone this time before it went to voicemail. Hello, I said. Reggie said, I called you earlier. I thought you would have already been home. I told him there was a little situation on our way home. He asked, why didn't you call me when you got in? I looked at the phone receiver and thought, what the hell? Did he not just hear me say there was a situation? In my sarcastic tone, Al and I are fine; thank you for asking. I thought, I don't believe in much drama, but pretend like you care. Red Flag number one – he is not concerned about what I dealt with. I did not even know I had been analyzing this conversation for so long that I didn't hear Reggie call me. Parris, Parris.

I responded, oh, I am sorry; I wasn't listening closely to you; I was dwelling on your insensitivity. I would not have been so direct if I had not let Mi-Mi's words linger in my head. Here comes Al to save the day. Tapping me on the arm, Mommy, Mommy, who are you talking to? Is that Mr. Reggie? Before I could answer, he grabbed the phone's receiver and said, "Hi, Mr. Reggie. After Al took the receiver, there was two-year-old gibberish that neither Reggie nor I understood. As I took the receiver back, I could hear Reggie laughing. I guess Reggie got over the fact that I had not called him when I got home. I wrestled internally in my head over the next few days. Although it was difficult, I eventually put Mi-Mi's comment to the back of my mind and continued to talk to Reggie two to three times per day.

CHAPTER 17

Oh No You Didn't

We took a trip to Las Vegas, Nevada - the first real vacation I had taken since Al was born. I was so excited to spend time with Reggie for an entire week. Reggie flew into Dulles Airport, and I picked him up. Al was glad to see him. Al started jumping up and down and running around as if he had a few cups of coffee. I had my two men with me. Reggie, Al, and I went to dinner and returned to my apartment a little after 8 pm. Since Al has his own bathroom, I got Al in and out of the bathtub while Reggie showered in my bathroom. Reggie insisted on tucking Al into bed. While Reggie read Al a bedtime story, I jumped in the shower. I could not fall asleep, anticipating our upcoming trip.

I lay down in the bed next to Reggie. I was the only one who could not sleep. Reggie was calling the hogs, as my grandma would say. By the time I got to sleep, the alarm clock was going off. I desperately wanted to hit the snooze button but did not want to oversleep. Before waking up Al, I ensured I had packed and put our suitcases in the car. When I came back in, Reggie was on the phone. I side-eyed him, and he knew what that look meant because he put his hand over the receiver and said, I am telling my mother goodbye before we get on the road. I whispered back, tell her I said hello. I am going to get Al dressed. I thought it was a sweet gesture seeing Reggie keep in touch with his mother; how a man treats his mother is how he would treat his significant other, so I thought. A relationship is headed towards disaster if the momma's boy does not end his co-dependent relationship with his mother. As time was ticking and Al and I were ready and waiting, Reggie was still on the phone with his mother – Red Flag # 2. I pointed to my watch, and he put up his pointer finger, signifying me to wait one minute. If this dude does not come on, we will never make it to the airport on time. We still have to drop off Al with my sister and brother-in-law. Another few minutes passed; I looked at Reggie; we were cutting it close because we were flying out of Baltimore Washington International Airport. Thankfully, Yvette's and John's apartment was en route to the airport. Reggie said we should be okay getting to the airport on time. I told him we had to get on the BW Parkway, and there was no telling how heavy the traffic would be on the way to the airport. We still have to park, get a shuttle to the airport, get our boarding passes, get through security, and get to the gate.

CHAPTER 18

Who Am I Vacationing With?

It was an intense ride to the airport. I was heated because we only had thirty minutes to get to the gate after we dropped off Al and made it to security. We got to the gate as the door closed. We could still see the plane; it had not pulled away from the gate, but the airline representative advised us they were not permitted to open the door once it had been closed. We would have to take the next flight, which was four hours from then. Reggie slammed his suitcase down, looked at me, and yelled at the top of his lungs – This is all your fault! You made us miss the flight!

Reggie, I kept telling you to come on, but you would not get off the phone with your mother. My mother has nothing to do with this. It is your fault. Instead of standing there continuing to go back and forth with him, I looked at him and walked away. Knowing integrity is based on what I will not do; I refused to stand in the middle of an airport arguing when I knew I was not to blame. When I walked away, I made sure not to turn around. I left him in the middle of the airport, looking foolish as security walked towards him. What is it with me having these interactions with these men in the middle of the airport?

I shuttled back to my car with tears in my eyes. I returned to my sister's apartment when my brother-in-law asked what had happened and where Reggie was. After I told them what happened, their phone rang. Surprise, surprise. My brother-in-law answered the phone and not in a happy way. He said Reggie, my little sister, told me what had happened. Whether or not she wants to continue this trip is up to her. John told Reggie that if she comes to us again with tears in her eyes because of you disrespecting her, you and I will communicate man-to-man. Then John handed me the receiver. When I said hello, he first said, I am sorry. He asked me if I would please go with him to Vegas so he could make it up to me. When I got off the phone, John and Yvette were cracking up laughing. I asked them what I had missed. They said they could not believe I had left him at the airport.

CHAPTER 19

No words

I returned to the airport two hours before the flight left. Reggie saw me, dropped his head, and apologized again. I was happy to be on vacation but not too excited with the person I was with. There was some tension in the air as we flew into Harry Reid International Airport. I became increasingly excited as we rode in a taxi to the hotel. I will give Reggie his kudos. He booked a room at The Mandalay Bay Resort and Casino. When we got to the room, I was amazed. The floor-to-ceiling windows, the stone surfaces, and the full view of the strip blew me away. I stood at the window until I heard talking. I asked him if he had said something. Red Flag #3 When I turned around, he was on the phone. I was hoping he was ordering room service because I was so hungry.

NOPE; he was on the phone with... that woman. He had not learned from our past experience. I looked at him, rolled my eyes, picked up one of the room keys, and walked down to the casino. I started wondering if he was really talking to his mother or if he was talking to another female while he was with me. Was he talking to his former fiancé? Was she actually a "former," or were they reconciling? I walked around the casino for about forty-five minutes, deciding whether to return home or enjoy my time in Vegas. What have I gotten myself into? One hundred thirty-five thousand freaking square feet of casino, and fortuitously, I walked right into Reggie.

Was I just tired and making more out of what was there? Reggie grabbed my hand and held it. He said I was just letting my mother know we made it safely. I cannot blame him; I wanted to call Al to check on him, but after getting upset with Reggie for being on the phone, I dared not call him. I knew he was in good hands, so I relaxed and enjoyed the next three days. Reggie and I held hands and walked the strip at 11:30 at night. It was remarkable how many people walked around like it was daytime. I see why Las Vegas is called the city that never sleeps. We walked past the Bellagio on the way back to our hotel room. I was mesmerized by the fountain's performance. Once the performance ended, we continued to our hotel, which was only a few blocks away. We finally returned to our hotel room, showered, lay in bed, and talked.

CHAPTER 20

It All Makes Sense Now

We never discussed what happened at the airport, but he finally told me about his family. His mother was his biggest supporter – I was not surprised by that. His mother was married twice. His first stepfather, according to Reggie, was violent and abusive to Reggie and Reggie's mother. Reggie has two brothers – both younger than him. He did not know his biological father. When Reggie told me that, my heart sank. I saw his face become deeply sorrowful. I asked him if his father was still alive. He said yes, he lives in Tampa with his two children. So, are those your two younger brothers? No, my father has one daughter he is not in touch with. She is my age, and he has one son and one daughter with his first wife. My two brothers are from my mother. So, are you the oldest out of the six of you? He nodded and said yes.

I held Reggie closer because he had a face of defeat. Reggie told me that both of his brothers are married and have children. He told me his grandmother raised him for the first four years because his mother had him at the age of seventeen, and his mother was not prepared to raise a baby. I told Reggie we do have something in common. My mother had my sister at seventeen and had me when she was eighteen. I thought the only difference between our mothers was that my mother raised my sister and Me. My mother got married right before my sister was born. To no surprise, that did not last. Reggie chuckled. Yeah, I think that's what they did back then - the girl gets pregnant, you usually have to marry her. I agree. I guess families were always worried about upholding reputations. I do not believe the answer to an unplanned pregnancy is marriage. I asked Reggie if his father married his mother or his sister's mother. Again, looking defeated, he said no. I felt so badly for him.

I let him know my mother was seventeen years old - getting married to a guy who was leaving for the Air Force. Thankfully, my mother could stay with her in-laws while her husband left for the military. Who would have thought I would be born one year and six months after my sister was born? Throughout my early years, I knew I was not the golden child. Reggie said, well, I guess not only did our mothers have us early, but neither of us was our mother's favorite.

I asked Reggie; why do you think you were not your mom's favorite? I have a brother, Xavier, and it does not matter what he does; my mother coddles him. I don't know why my mother cannot see through his b.s. I think it's because his father died in an accident while she was pregnant with him, and she was head over heels in love with him. She probably feels sorry for Xavier, her only son who did not have the opportunity to grow up with his biological father. Xavier has three kids - that we know of. He said his brother is known to come to town and not tell anyone he is there, and all his mother says when she finds out is, "You know how he is." I have a question, but I do not want to offend you. When Reggie said to ask away, I felt at ease.

If your mother is so attached to your brother, why are you so attached to your mother? I know it's your mother, but are all three of you as close to your mother as you? Before he could answer me, I was answering in my head. Was it because he was so thirsty for attention from his mother? Was it because he wanted a mother-son relationship like his brother has with his mother? Or is this how he handles rejection from family members – he moves closer to try and establish the type of relationship he desires? It takes Reggie a while to answer my question. While waiting for his answer, I have all kinds of sidebars in my head. I am mentally documenting all sorts of red flags. Then, I have to regroup. Matthew 7:1-2 *"Judge not, that ye be judged. For with that judgment, ye judge, ye shall be judged: and with what measure ye mete, it shall be measured to you again.* This is what Jesus is commanding. I am not the one to judge anyone's upbringing. Look at how jacked up mine was.

We held each other after we shared more stories. I concluded we had more in common than I thought. Not that what we had in common was good or emotionally enlightening; it explained some of the behavior I had seen from Reggie. Nonetheless, we grew closer that night. It was no longer a matter of trying to impress one another. We had discussed areas in our lives that showed some of our vulnerabilities.

That morning, we got up and got ready for the breakfast buffet at the Mandalay Bay's restaurant. Next, we strolled the strip, taking in the sights, and Lord knows there were some sights to take in. I looked up at one of the marquees. I could not believe it, Donna Summer. I told him she was one of my favorite performers. Reggie said we can go. I told him I know we did not come to Vegas to go to a concert. Reggie said, " If that will make you happy, let's do it. I was so excited until I saw that her performance would not be until the day after we left. Reggie said we should extend our vacation so I can attend the concert. We couldn't; I had to get Al as expected because my sister had plans. I held him even tighter, knowing Reggie wanted to make me happy. I never got a chance to see Donna Summer live in concert. She passed away from cancer in 2012.

CHAPTER 21

A Good Time Misinterpreted

What transpired between Reggie and me at the airport on the way to Vegas was in the back of my mind. Even though Reggie's blow-up scared me, and for many women, that would have been the end. If that had not happened to me, I would say the same thing – girl, you need to leave that man; don't stick around waiting for it to happen again; you need to care more about yourself; what if he doesn't change; what kind of example are you setting for your child?

Over the past couple of days, I have seen a different, more vulnerable side of Reggie. He opened up, allowing me to see his hurt. Yes, I have had hurt and rejection, too, and I have not lashed out in the manner he did. That is not to say I have handled my pain in a godly way; I just chose a different way of handling it. Ephesians 4:26 *Be ye angry, and sin not: let not the sun go down upon your wrath* – so since I know better, I pray to do better. I heard Dr. Jasmin Sculark, a phenomenal minister, say that just because I am a Christian does not mean I am sinless. It just means that I sin less. I try to take that to heart for anyone I encounter. Why should I expect others to be perfect when I am so far from ideal?

For the next day or two, I have been praying for revelation. Is this relationship just like bread, milk, and eggs; is there an expiration date, or will this be something that blossoms into forever? We enjoyed ourselves immensely for the remaining time we were there. We visited several different hotels. We walked the strip and enjoyed each other's company. After a few more days of fun, we were on our way back to Virginia. We made it back to BWI Airport and picked up Al. After talking to my sister and brother-in-law for a while, we headed back to my apartment. We talked a little but mostly listened to Al talk about everything he did with Auntie and Uncle. Al spoke so fast from the excitement of telling us what he had done with his Aunt, Uncle, and cousins. I had no idea half what he said, but I smiled and nodded, and he was okay with that.

CHAPTER 22

Three Weeks Later and I Am All Alone - AGAIN

When we returned to my apartment, we ordered dinner and watched TV. As soon as Al was tucked in and asleep, Reggie walked up to me and kissed me so passionately that I wanted to melt. When we finally pulled ourselves away from one another, I asked him what that was for. He said for loving me. I asked, for loving you? Who said anything about me loving you? He said, well, from the smile on your face, you are still speaking to me after I acted like a fool on the way to Vegas. He held me closer and said, I am so sorry. You did not deserve that. I thought to myself again; he did not say he would not do it again. I will have to keep that in mind. I will not allow my internal conversations to ruin this last evening together. Thank you for loving me enough to apologize, I said. He smiled and kissed me again.

The next day, I dropped him off at the airport and kissed him goodbye. I am unsure what happened between that last kiss and the two days later. I had yet to hear from Reggie other than letting me know he made it safely back to Atlanta and how much of a good time he had. I got no returned trouble tickets or phone calls for the next three weeks - this was strange. Either I am doing my work 100% correctly, or something has happened. When we did converse, it was all business. When he did call to discuss any tickets, they weren't mine. I just happened to be available in the queue to answer the call. I answered, and there was a pause on the line, causing me to introduce myself twice. Thank you for calling Telecom Services; how can I help you? Um, yeah, I have a ticket that needs reviewing. I followed his lead regarding the flat tone – um, yeah, what is the ticket number? He provided the ticket number; I thanked him and told him to have a good day, said goodbye, and hung up. The entire time I talked to him, I had butterflies. Over the past six to eight months, I had fallen in love with this man. What happened in forty-eight hours that turned our relationship upside down?

CHAPTER 23

Get Your Arrogance in Check

A week later, I went to work only to find a letter on my desk. I was so terrified to open it. My desk was the only desk with a letter. Did Raymond's idiotic girlfriend get me fired? I opened it slowly. Congratulations, you have been selected for a second interview for a Technical Support position based in Atlanta, GA.

My eyes read this letter over and over and over again. It did not seem real until my director came and congratulated me. HR sends the letter sealed, so how did my director know I had an interview? Oh yeah, this is corporate; nothing is secret. My jaws were hurting from smiling for so long. Then the call came in: Hi, Parris. It's Reggie; there is a ticket that needs addressing. I wanted to tell him so desperately that he helped me get an interview until I heard how he addressed me. Can you look at this ticket and then send it back? I asked him what was wrong with the ticket, and he suggested I review and correct it. I will be waiting for it to come back. I said, thank you – have a good day and I hung up. When I heard my personal line ring, I knew exactly who it was.

I did not feel like answering his call and subjecting myself to arrogance; however, this was part of my job, so I answered the call – This is Parris. Hey Parris, are you okay? Psalm 39:1 *I will take heed to my ways, that I sin not with my tongue: I will keep my mouth with a bridle, while the wicked is before me.* Hi Reggie,

I am doing well. How are you? He said I am doing pretty good; you seemed bothered when I sent the ticket back for review. How about you call me this evening, and we can discuss it? I don't want to talk about it on a recorded line. Okay, I will speak with you this evening. We said our goodbyes and hung up. I was so excited when I got off. I rushed to get Al, and then I went home. I had the interview tomorrow, and Reggie was supposed to call this evening.

I don't think Al and I were in the house for over five minutes when the phone rang. Hello? Hey Parris, it's Reggie. I said, hello, how are you? He said, I am fine - What's going on with you? Not much. Knowing we would keep going back and forth with small talk, I eventually said, Reggie, I wanted to talk to you regarding your handling of tickets. Your tone towards me and others seems aggressive. I know we don't always do things correctly. Still, we don't purposely sit around the office and think of ways to do things incorrectly to make your life difficult. I cannot believe I got all that out without him interrupting me. I said, Reggie? He was so quiet that I thought maybe he had hung up. I am still here. I did not want to interrupt you if you had more to say. I told him I was finished. He began to apologize for coming across as combative. I was shocked. Did Reggie apologize to me? I started to let my guard down. That is one of my most significant flaws; I accept apologies and forgive quickly.

Reggie, I received a letter at work today. It was a letter about the position I applied for. He said; Uh huh. I have an interview tomorrow. He asked, tomorrow? They don't give you enough time to prepare. Well, that is where you come in, Reggie. I wanted to thank you for all of your preparation. All of the help you gave me. The mock interviews you worked with me on. I appreciate it all. Parris, you are welcome. I am glad I was able to help. I let him know I would call him after the interview. Reggie encouraged me by reassuring me I would do well. Just think, when you get the job, you and Al will be with me.

I was beyond confused. Were we or were we not a couple? We have not spoken in over two weeks. Is this the way he thinks couples communicate? I thought maybe he had gone back to his ex-fiancé. Reggie brought me out of my trance when he said, Parris, are you okay? Oh yes. I am good. I was thinking about us all being together again. I am looking forward to it. Al interrupted our conversation. Mommy, I am hungry. Well, let me get off the phone. I will talk to you later. Have a good night. Reggie said okay, you too and we hung up.

CHAPTER 24

From The DMV To The "A"

Well, I am back home—well, sort of. I just arrived back in Georgia. The DMV (D.C., Maryland, Virginia) will always be my home. The DMV offers crabs by the bushel, Hanes Point, Go-Go, Half Smokes, Ben's Chili Bowl, Chicken Wings, and Mambo sauce, but returning to Atlanta felt good. My family's roots started in Watkinsville, Oconee, Georgia. So, I guess I was sort of back home.

I was so excited to be in the training class on day one. What in the hell? Reggie walked into the training class. Mi-Mi, the one from my previous job in Virginia, walked in right behind Reggie. Okay, Lord, what in the world is going on? I thought this would be a new start, not a new start with the same people. Reggie looked directly at me and walked past me. Oh no, he didn't – okay; this is how we will do this? Mi-Mi, being the messy person she is, smiled and said, hi Parris. Aren't you and Reggie going to sit together? I looked at her and said, hello, Mi-Mi. She walked over to Reggie and said, hi, Reggie, I didn't know you were going to work in Tech Support; the entire time, she was looking in my direction. Reggie smiled at her. I had no idea they were on speaking terms enough with one another enough to converse. Mi-Mi is the same person who told me I should not trust Reggie. I no longer felt butterflies in my stomach when I saw or talked to Reggie. I now have a sinking in the pit of my stomach when he is around.

The class had started, and it was now time for introductions. Why do training representatives think this is so necessary? We will not remember each other's name or previous position – nor do I care to know. There were about two people ahead of me introducing themselves. I excused myself and went to the restroom. I waited until I knew the trainer had moved on past the introductions. I started walking back to the training class. I saw Reggie walking towards me. Hi Reggie, how are you? Hi Parris. I am fine. We kept walking in opposite directions. That was awkward. What happened? Why did we stop talking? He was looking and smelling good. I knew that cologne quite well. It was Davidoff's Cool Water for Men. Lord, give me strength to leave this man alone. I was good for about two weeks. I was thinking, okay, maybe I can get through this.

During a break, I walked outside to take a deep breath to avoid my sadness showing. Reggie walked out right behind me. I thought I heard him call me, but I was unsure, so I did not embarrass myself; I kept walking. Parris, Parris. I slowed down and turned around. Reggie was literally in my face. Surprisingly, he jogged to catch up to me. I am sorry, Reggie; I was in a daze. Reggie asked how I was doing. I am fine, how are you? I am fine, he replied.

CHAPTER 25

Reconciling After Not Breaking Up?

I have been watching you, Parris. I giggled and said, I know. That's kind of stalkerish, don't you think? We both laughed. Reggie had broken the ice. He leaned in and hugged me, not a church hug, but a romantic hug. I did not want to let go. He smelled so good, and I felt so safe in his arms. As we both let go of each other, we started to lean in for a kiss until one of our classmates walked up behind us, reminding us that we would be late getting back from break if we waited any longer. We both looked at our watches and hurried upstairs to the classroom. We were late. The instructor had a rule. You must sing a song if you are late returning from break or lunch. Reggie sang Bad to the Bone. I sang Tramaine Hawkins' song "What Shall I Do?" While it was a fun requirement to get into the class late, I was actually singing to the Lord, asking for guidance as it related to Reggie and My relationship. "What shall I do? What step should I take? What move shall I make? Oh Lord, what shall I do? I'm going to wait. For I know You'll come through." The class' standing ovation brought me back to reality.

When it was time for lunch, I went outside to enjoy the quiet, peaceful time. Reggie pulled up in his Prelude and asked if I was going to eat lunch. I told him no; I didn't bring anything and was not hungry. He asked me if I would accompany him to lunch. I figured I might as well. What else was there to do? We went to his place, which was only five to ten minutes away from the job. Ten minutes if he missed the light at Cumberland Parkway. We had forty-five minutes left before we had to go back to work. He fixed himself a sandwich and asked if I wanted anything. I only wanted something to drink. After he finished eating, I leaned on his shoulder, and he lowered his head and kissed me on my cheek. He said I have missed you so much. I told him I missed him too. What happened, Reggie? Why did we stop talking? We need to make sure we continue to communicate. I don't want the lack of communication to end our relationship. If we are in a relationship? I made that statement but also stated it as a question. He looked at me and said yes, we are in a relationship.

CHAPTER 26

Ana's Short-Lived Acceptance

I finally met Parris. Reggie would not stop talking about her. He talked about how pretty and how smart she was. Parris is a beautiful young lady with a beautiful spirit. My son has always been attracted to plus-size women, and she fits in that category. Parris seems to love my son. I wonder if he told her about his upbringing, whether or not she is a Christian, and what drew my son to her. I have so many questions I want to ask. When she and her son came in, I could tell she was a bit nervous, especially when Reggie left her with the women, and he went with the men downstairs. Her son enjoys being with Reggie. He follows Reggie around like a little puppy. Reggie has no children and has never dated a woman with children, so this is new to him. I hope he knows what he is doing and does not live his past in his present.

I walked over to Parris and sat beside her so she could feel more comfortable. I could tell she was uneasy because when she glanced at me, she had a somewhat startled look on her face. I hugged her and told her I was delighted to meet her finally. I told her I look forward to spending more time with her and Al. Her face softened, and she smiled. Reggie returned to what I call the women's section to check on Parris. I told Reggie she was okay. I told him to go back with the men. Reggie smiled, kissed Parris, and went back downstairs with the men. The way Reggie and Parris looked at one another, I could tell there was love between them. I know they have just started dating, so it is too soon to say whether or not this love will last beyond dating. Reggie's former girlfriend, who turned into a former fiancé, left him hurt beyond what you would want to see your child endure. Reggie's ex-fiancé called off their wedding after Reggie paid a down payment on a venue for the wedding and reception. Reggie had also lost money he put towards a house they were supposed to move into after marriage. I pray Reggie's hatred towards his ex-fiancé will not be reflected in his relationship with Parris. I hope this is not a rebound relationship because a child has lovingly become attached to Reggie. Even though I am not ready to give my son to another woman – again, I will continue to pray that the three of them remain happy together.

Reggie came upstairs with Al behind him, whining. Reggie told me it was time to go because Al was tired and needed to nap. Parris gathered their things while Reggie took Al to the car and strapped him in his car seat. Parris hugged me goodbye and told all the women it was nice meeting them. She hurried to the car before realizing she grabbed everything except her purse.

CHAPTER 27

You Like Me, They Like Me Not

As I approached the car, I turned around to return to the house. I overheard Reggie's mother saying how much she liked me and that she had not seen her son this happy in quite a while. That made me smile until I heard Reggie's cousin say, I am still trying to figure her out. I am not sure if I like her or not. As I opened the door, all the women in the room looked in my direction. They stared at me as if they saw a deer caught in the headlights. They knew I heard what his cousin said. I walked into the house with my head held high – as if I owned the house. Reggie's mother asked me if we were okay. I told her, yes, I forgot my purse.

My mind was full of racing thoughts that did not represent God in any way. Knowing when to flip the script and go from good to hood was always challenging. I usually respond quickly to negative comments about me - this is a self-protection mechanism, not allowing others to run over me. However, this time, I kept somewhat quiet, trying to maintain my composure as best as possible. I told the ladies goodbye again. With my eyes closed to a slit and the corner of my mouth raised, I looked Reggie's cousin directly in her eyes and said, it was nice meeting you. I hope we can get to know each other so that you can learn more about me and I can learn more about you. Of course, I was being acerbic. It felt so good to let her know – winch, I heard you, without saying winch, I heard you. As I walked out of the door again the same way I came in, with my head held up high, you could hear a pin drop. Thank God they did not see me trip down the last step. There was one doggone step – GEESH. When I got to the car, Reggie was laughing at me. I put on my fly sunglasses, clicked on my seatbelt, pulled down the visor, opened the mirror, checked my hair and makeup, looked at Reggie, and said; and I still look good. We both laughed.

Al and I went to Reggie's place before going home. His mother called about fifteen minutes after we got to Reggie's apartment. I was sure she could not wait to tell him what transpired between his cousin and me. I had not said anything about what I heard from his cousin's mouth. I didn't say anything because I did not want Reggie to know what was said and because I was in too much pain from tripping. By the time we got to Reggie's place, I could barely walk on my foot. My ankle was so swollen that Reggie asked if I wanted to go to the doctor. While Reggie was on the phone with his mother, he kept glancing in my direction. All I could think was this night was not going to end well. He glanced at me again before hanging up with his mother.

I could not figure out what they were talking about. While I was ear-hustling, I only heard Reggie say, no; when did that happen? Really? Not one word, okay, love you too, momma, and then he hung up. He came and sat next to me on the sofa. I asked him if anything was wrong. He said so; what happened at my aunt's house today? I just stared at him, trying to figure out what the mouth of the South told him. I told him what I heard his cousin say when I returned to the house to get my purse. He asked what I said. I told him I could not believe he was taking sides this early in our relationship. Was I supposed to not respond to his cousin?

I went through the entire scenario of what happened. Reggie did not interrupt me once while I was talking. That stirred up nervousness because all he does is interrupt when he disagrees. I wondered if he was too upset with me to interrupt or if he agreed with what I said to his cousin. I got my answer when I finished speaking. Reggie asked me if I was ready for him to take Al and Me home. My answer, yes, was stuck in my throat and came out as a whisper. It was difficult for me to hold back the tears. I limped to the restroom and splashed some water on my face to hide the tears so that Al did not notice me crying.

The fifteen-minute ride home felt more like hours. Neither of us said anything until we got to my apartment. Reggie got Al out of his car seat and put the car seat into my car, reminding me to fasten it before I put Al in the car seat. Reggie took Al into his room, tucked him into bed, and then started to leave. I asked him if he would like to stay and talk. When he said no, I just stared at him and said good night. Please be careful getting home and let me know when you get in. He walked out of the door. I wanted to kiss him goodbye, but he did not tell me goodbye until he was almost in his car. Reggie let me know he made it home safely. I thought everything would be okay, but he did not answer my phone calls for the remainder of the weekend. I stopped calling.

CHAPTER 28

Why Can't She Read My Mind?

Again, another two weeks with no conversation. It was so bothersome. Except for Reggie's cousin, I enjoyed the uniqueness of his family – four generations of love. My upbringing was mostly my mom, dad, and sister; some holidays were spent with my grandparents, an aunt, an uncle, and a cousin.

I thought I had found the one – brains and beauty inside and out. Why didn't Parris just ignore my cousin? Of course, my mother timed my ride home perfectly to make sure she called to tell me what had happened when I got in the house. I cannot blame Parris for standing up for herself, but not on the first day of meeting my family. The tricky part is my mother loves Parris and enjoys being around her.

As the phone rings, Reggie hopes it's Parris. Oh, hi, Momma – Reggie sighs inside. No, momma, I have not heard from Parris. I saw her at work. Momma, I miss her, but I think she has already moved on. Reggie's mother chuckled. Reggie, why would you say that? It's only been two weeks. When we are at work, there is always one guy always in her face. They both giggle with one another. They go to lunch together, and he walks her to her car after our shift. Reggie's mother tells him that does not mean she is moving on; it just means she is communicating with a co-worker. If you don't speak up, Reggie, you will lose her. If you want her, let her know.

Reggie's call-waiting beeped. Momma, I will call you back. He clicks over and says, hello? One of his best friends wanted to know if he wanted to go out. Reggie said, sure, let me get dressed. Where do you want to go? The Spot Sports Bar and Grille on Flat Shoals in Decatur. Alright, man, I will see you at about 8. Are they showing the game? His friend said yup, I already checked. Reggie hung up and then started getting ready to go. After showering and getting dressed, he put on his cologne and headed out the door. Reggie saw his answer machine blinking, showing two unheard messages. Assuming the messages were from his mother and avoiding the disappointment of the messages not being from Parris, Reggie left without checking the messages, deciding he would check them when he got back home.

CHAPTER 29

How Did The Three Of Us End Up Here Together?

Reggie arrived at the Sports Bar and Grille and saw his boys at the bar, where he joined them to get the night started with a lot of fun and trash-talking. After being at the bar for about fifteen minutes, much to his surprise and disappointment, he saw Parris at the door with the guy from work. Reggie's heart sank. The server asked Parris and Raymond if the two of them wanted a booth or a table. Reggie's mind started racing. If they get a booth, the two of them are more than friends; if they sit at a table, they are just hanging out. Raymond asked for a booth. Parris quickly corrected him and said a table would be fine. YES, Reggie shouted out loud. His boys looked at him with a perplexed look. They followed Reggie's gaze and were even more perplexed seeing Parris sitting at a table with some man.

Reggie told his boys he was coming over to the table to speak. Nervously, Reggie approached the table with his hands in his pocket. Parris's beautiful smile set him at ease. She said, Reggie, would you like to have a seat? Parris's hangout buddy frowned when Reggie accepted. Reggie told them he couldn't stay at the table long because he was with some friends. Thirty minutes later, Reggie reluctantly returned to the bar with his boys but smiled for the remainder of the night, stealing glances at Parris while she also stole glances at him.

I wonder why Parris didn't want to sit at the booth. Was it too intimate? Our table was finally ready, and as we sat down, I spotted Reggie from work. I know Reggie and Parris used to date, so I stepped up my game by pulling out Parris's chair with a smile as I got a whiff of her perfume. She always smells good. I hope we can take this up a notch and that she will agree to be with me exclusively. Oh no, this dude is not coming over here. This rude m.f. - did Parris invite him to sit down? What in the hell is going on? I was not just mad; I was peeved.

I keep glancing at her so she knows I am not happy. She won't even look my way – she is just skinning and grinning in this dude's face. Let me get myself together. Let me regain my composure. I don't want to come across to Parris as an egotistical hothead. I have been working with her for a few months now, and she is not the type of woman who would accept any type of diabolical behavior.

She is intelligent and beautiful and always has a smile on her face. She has two dimples below each corner of her mouth. Her dimples seem more profound when she smiles or laughs, making me stare at her even more.

The one thing I will have to get used to is her son. She has a two or three-year-old. He is adorable, but usually, women with children have turned me off. Parris may be the exception; she takes such good care of him and herself. I picked her up from her house. Her home was bigger than expected, especially since it was just the two of them. I was looking forward to meeting her son, but Parris did not want to introduce her son to any of her male friends. She is definitely raising him the right way. She had her Associate's, Bachelor's, and Master's degrees framed and hanging on her wall - brains, beauty, and confidence.

It's been thirty minutes, and Reggie is still at our table. I will sit back and enjoy the game or at least pretend like I am enjoying the game. Our food and drinks came, and Reggie finally left to return to the bar. We ordered wings and fries. I ordered a drink and was not surprised when Parris ordered a Diet Coke. That is what she always drinks at work.

CHAPTER 30

It's A Date, It's Not A Date

When Raymond and I entered the bar and grille, I could not believe Reggie was there. I saw the hurt on his face when he saw me with Raymond. What an uncomfortable situation. Me being out with a mutual co-worker only a couple of weeks after we ceased communication. I desperately wanted to hug and kiss Reggie. Then I saw the look on Raymond's face. After Raymond and I were seated, Reggie approached the table. Raymond's expression went from a smile to an aggressive sneer. I thought Reggie would just speak and return to the bar with his friends. When he sat down at our table, Raymond's face became contorted. All I could think was that they would get into an altercation. They both tried to hold their composure. As much as I wanted Reggie to stay, I was glad he returned to the bar. I was starting to softly hum the song by Anita Baker and the Winans – "Ain't no need to worry, what the night is going to bring, it will be all over in the morning."

After we ate, we talked for the next hour or so. I knew I had a jewel, and she would demand that I treat her as such. We exchanged stories of our upbringing – I am from Atlanta, Georgia; she is from Washington, D.C. I have two older sisters and one younger brother. She has three older sisters, one older brother, and one younger brother. So, Parris, do all of your siblings live in D.C.? No. I have a brother in Charlotte, NC, and the other siblings are in the

DMV area. What was it like growing up with all of those siblings? I only grew up with one of my older sisters. We all have different mothers, except for the sister I grew up with. She said her mother and step-up father raised her and her sister. I asked, your step-up father? That's a new one to me. She said that although most men can create babies, raising a child takes a real father or step-up father. She told me her step-up father was the most important man in her life. He raised her and her sister as his own; although he and her mother are now divorced, he still cares for them and the grandkids. She said, now that is a man and a father.

She told me she met her older and younger brother recently. She loved both of her brothers tremendously. She met the other two sisters, but they shunned her. I nearly fell out of my chair. Parris told me she experienced one of the most unfathomable hurts in her life, finding out she had four additional siblings. Her life changed overnight. Parris had been through some stuff. The way Parris represents herself, I could not tell she endured so much. Any man should be happy to have her on his arm. I will work at making her my queen as long as I can keep Reggie out of her face.

After Reggie left our table, Parris became distant. She pretended to be watching the game, but I knew better, so I asked her if she was ready to leave. Glancing at her watch, she said yes. She told me now would be a good time to leave since we had to work the first shift. I asked the waitress for a to-go box for Parris' wings and the check. I think I was just as ready to leave as Parris.

CHAPTER 31

Silence Is Not Golden

I dreaded the ride home. I knew Raymond was upset that Reggie spent much of our outing at our table. After Raymond paid the bill, we got up and headed to the door. I glanced at Reggie and said goodbye to him with my eyes. Reggie saw us leaving and gave us a head nod goodbye. As we got to Raymond's car, I heard Reggie say, Parris, you forgot your food. I am always forgetting something. I took the container from Reggie, and our hands touched. It was electrifying. We made eye contact for about two seconds too long before Raymond asked me if I was ready to go. I got in Raymond's car. When I buckled my seatbelt, Raymond asked me if I wanted Reggie to take me home. I looked at Raymond and said, Reggie was bringing me the food I left on the table.

I am glad he did because this will be my lunch tomorrow. I tried to lessen the tension in the air, but that didn't work. What an unpleasantly quiet thirty-minute ride home. I tried to engage Raymond in conversation, but he was not hearing it. Generally, I can come up with some topic for small talk, but, after Raymond shunned my first attempt. I did not make any more attempts. I kept thinking about Reggie and how I felt when his hand touched mine. We finally got on my street. I started taking off my seatbelt as Raymond approached the front of my house. I was so glad to be back home. I thanked him for the evening, told him to drive safely, and let me know when he got home. He looked at me, backed out of the driveway, and was gone before I reached the front door. That was enough for me to know Raymond was not the man for me. He messed that up when he put his vehicle in reverse and stepped on the gas before he knew I was safely in my house.

Oh well, now that that is over. Should I call Reggie or let him call me? I do not like to play games, but do I want to take the chance of being rejected? That would hurt me – again. I got in the shower and got ready for bed. I tried to read Casting the First Stone by Kimberla Lawson Roby. I read the same paragraph at least three times before I put the book down. All I could think about was Reggie and what tomorrow would be like at work. I am not a fan of foolishness, but if I were a psychic and could see into the future, I would see a complete day of chaos.

CHAPTER 32

I Thought Drama Was A Female Thang'
As always, I am at work twenty minutes early. I prepare my tea and make sure my makeup is applied evenly. The women's bathroom light is always much brighter than at home. After checking my makeup, I return to my desk, sit down, and prepare to start a new day.

Good morning, Parris. Good morning, Reggie; how are you? Pretty good. I asked Parris if we could go to lunch to discuss last night's awkwardness. Parris said we could go to lunch, but we did not have to discuss last night unless you had something to say. I will listen to you, but I prefer to forget last night. I raised my eyebrows at Parris in surprise. For the first time in my life, I was speechless. I continued to stare into Parris' eyes as if she would answer questions I had not come up with yet.

Raymond came in like a punk, looking at both of us and rolling his eyes. Parris sighed and sat back in her chair. She asked me to get logged in and meet her downstairs to go and get breakfast. I accommodated her request with a smile on my face. I wondered if she wanted breakfast or if she wanted to talk. I could not help but smirk as I walked past Raymond. He glared at me – if looks could kill, I would be six feet under. I logged in and met Parris downstairs. I guess she didn't want him to see us walk downstairs together. As we walked to the cafeteria, she gave me the entire story of Raymond's quiet rant. Parris described how Raymond dropped her off at home and did not wait for her to get into her house before leaving. She said he did not even wait for her to get to her door. What kind of mess is that? What if she never made it inside? There are so many what-ifs.

Parris and I made it back to the office. Raymond was not getting any work done because he continued his piercing stares, glancing at Parris and then at me. Raymond's pettiness went on so long that Parris sent me an inter-office message telling me she was uncomfortable with what was happening. She said she was leaving early and asked if I would walk her to her car. I decided to take off the rest of the day, too. As we started walking to our cars, we saw Raymond following us. I told Parris to go to her vehicle and that I would follow her home to make sure no shenanigans popped off. Parris looked at me with the most sincere thank you.

CHAPTER 33

The Green-Eyed Monster Has A Gun

I was jolted back to reality when Raymond said, so, you all are taking off together? Thankfully, his manager followed him, asking him if everything was ok. Raymond looked between Parris and me and said, "Yeah, everything is okay – under his breath and only loud enough for me to hear "for now." I asked him what that meant. He just walked off with his manager. Parris drove to where I was parked and asked if I was ready. I am right behind you, I told her. I got in the Prelude and made sure to follow her closely. We arrived at her home. She has a two-car garage and a driveway that will fit six cars. She pulled up to the garage but didn't park in her garage. I started to park on the street, but she told me to pull into her driveway and park behind her. I parked and walked her to her door. I was surprised but grateful when she invited me in. I could tell she had been crying. I walked up to her until we were face to face, and then I wrapped my arms around her. Don't worry, Parris; I will make sure you are okay. She looked at me as if she wanted to believe me but was unsure. I asked her if she needed anything before I left. She leaned in and kissed me on my cheek. I should be okay, she said. Thank you so much for making sure I got in the house safely. Let me know when you get home. As Parris and I walked to the door, it was my turn to lean in and kiss her, and then we told each other goodbye.

I did not know that goodbye was potentially the last goodbye. Parris opened the door for me and saw a car across the street that resembled Raymond's vehicle. She quickly closed the door and asked me if that was Raymond's car. I wasn't sure because it was dark when I saw her get in his car last night. She looked out of the window and said, that is Raymond! She said she would call the police, but I told her nothing had happened that warranted a call to the police.

Please don't go outside; she was almost begging me. The fear in her eyes let me know I could not leave her alone. She started closing all of the blinds that would give anyone access to look into the house. I sat on the sofa and patted the spot next to me, asking her to sit down and relax. She sat down and handed me the TV remote control. She asked me if I wanted anything to eat or drink. That's when we heard her car alarm. She looked at me, ran to her front door, looked out of the peephole, and exclaimed, Jesus! That's when she saw the brick and most of the driver's side window on the ground. We both heard two gunshots, and a car sped off. She looked at me and said, can we call the police now?

CHAPTER 34

Is This The Wild, Wild West?

After the car sped off, Reggie and I went outside to see how much damage occurred to the vehicle. That's when I heard another two gunshots that seemed to be in the distance. After the brick through my window, gunshots, and a car speeding off, I called out for Reggie to call the police. As I called his name a couple of times and started running back to the house, thinking he had gone inside to call the police, I tripped and fell. I thought I would faint once I looked to see what I tripped over. Reggie was lying on the sidewalk, bleeding. I stayed on the ground next to him, putting pressure on the area where I saw blood flowing out. I yelled at no one in particular, someone, call 9-1-1. Please help me! Thankfully, two of my neighbors were retired and at home. One of my neighbors, a retired Army medic, helped me with Reggie, and my other neighbor was on the phone with a 9-1-1 dispatcher. The neighbor had the dispatcher on speakerphone, and the dispatcher kept asking what seemed to be pointless questions. While holding Reggie's head in my lap, I yelled, please send someone to help us. I kept letting Reggie know he would be okay.

Reggie closed his eyes, and my heart sank. I could hear the sirens in the background while Mr. Jay applied pressure on what we thought was the only wound. I said, Reggie, please hang on, baby, help is almost here. The scene quickly became more chaotic

- a firetruck, two police cars, and an ambulance. The paramedics took over while the police made me get up from Reggie. With tears in my eyes and not knowing Reggie's status, I was interrogated by two new officers who showed up. The officers asked me who lived at the residence. I told them I live here.

They went on to ask a ton of other questions. They wanted to know if Reggie lived here with me. They asked me if we were arguing or fighting before the shooting. Oh my God- "before the shooting." It is slowly registering; my house is a crime scene. The officers walked over to some detectives. I called my dad. My dad was a retired Washington, DC, police officer, and me being his baby girl. He will tell me exactly what to do and what to expect. The officers started yelling at me to get off the phone. My dad heard them and told me to put him on speakerphone. When I put him on speakerphone, I heard my dad say, this is retired DC Sr. Officer Snell. The officers lowered their voices as they spoke more civilly to my dad. One of the officers continued talking to my dad while another introduced me to a detective.

The detective asked me who lived at the residence and then asked if there had been any disagreements that occurred between the victim inside the house and me before the shooting. His name is Reggie. The detective stopped, looked at me, and began writing in his notepad. He asked if I knew Reggie's full name and whether we were friends or involved in a romantic relationship. As I was answering questions, I saw the paramedics putting electrodes on Reggie's chest.

The paramedics quickly put Reggie in the ambulance. I told the detectives and the officers I wanted to ride to the hospital with Reggie. The detectives told me they needed to finish their investigation, which included me going to the precinct to answer questions. I asked if I was being arrested. They looked at me and told me no, but they had more questions to ask me. I told them I have more answers for you, I am sure, but I am more interested in being by Reggie's side.

I asked the officers if I could go into the house to get showered. I had Reggie's blood all over my clothes and my hands. The officers tested my hands for gunpowder residue and then asked me if they could look around the inside and outside of the house for any clues. I told them that someone I care about tremendously could be dying, and I feel that you are accusing me of shooting him. I then told them, do what you must do so I can shower and get to the hospital. Please do not mess up my house with any Inspector Gadget shenanigans. I want to get to the hospital to check on Reggie.

The officers and the detectives walked into the house and quickly realized there was no crime scene inside the house. The only thing out of order was the two glasses of soda on the countertop. We never got to drink the soda because we heard the car alarm. The police and detectives searched the inside and outside of the house and finally left. Thankfully, I got one of my vehicles out of the garage since the other vehicle was part of the crime scene and unavailable. Oh, My Goodness – yellow crime scene tape. A freaking crime scene on Pamala Path. What in the world? As I sped towards the highway, attempting to get to Grady, one of the best trauma hospitals in Atlanta, I saw red brake lights.

CHAPTER 35

Drama Won't Leave Me Alone

I am over 24x7x365 rush hour traffic in Atlanta. I pulled into a gas station parking lot and entered Grady's address in the Waze app. Thankfully, Waze gives all of the back roads. I pull up to the hospital and immediately find a parking spot on the street. Learning to drive in Washington, D.C., most parking was street parking, giving me the advantage of knowing how to parallel park, making street parking quicker than pulling into a garage parking lot, pulling a ticket, and finding a space. I was able to park quickly and almost run to the emergency room. As I get to the receptionist's desk, I let the nurse know I am there for my fiancée, who was shot and should have arrived by ambulance a little over an hour ago.

The nurse turned and looked at me and put up her finger to indicate, wait a minute. She then turned and started to finish talking to her co-worker. I tried to get my mind together before jumping over this desk and looking for his information myself. She told her co-worker, "Girl, I haven't gone to lunch yet. Where is Nikki?" I politely said – okay, maybe not so politely – I don't care about your breaks, lunch, or start and finish times. Where is my fiancé? Yes, I was a little dishonest. I knew that if I said I was a co-worker, I would not be able to go to see Reggie. The look this girl gave me was priceless. After sucking her teeth and popping her gum one last time, she turned to her computer with nails about four inches long and eyelashes about the same length as her nails; she said with all of the attitude in the world – What is his name? I gave her his name, and she asked about my relationship with him. A little less than a yell – MY FIANCE!!!

I must have responded louder than I intended because the nurse's co-worker and others in the Emergency Room Waiting Room turned and looked at me. The security guard standing by the automatic doors started walking towards the counter, asking the nurse if she needed anything. Shouldn't he be asking me if I needed anything? I would be fine if she could tell me where I needed to go to get information regarding my fiancé. She finally advised that I needed to go to the trauma center. Go through the double doors and follow the directions to the trauma desk. All I could think was great, another desk. The nurse will be able to instruct you further. Humbling myself and with tears, I apologized for my outburst and being upset and told her thank you.

CHAPTER 36

Ana's Accusations Towards Parris

As I hurried through the doors and got to the trauma desk, I saw Reggie's family. Reggie's mother's eyes were red from her crying. I had the worst feeling in the pit of my stomach. Instead of asking the nurse for an update, I asked Reggie's mother what the doctors said.

I saw Parris walk off of the elevator. I glared at her and yelled at her - Reggie, being here is all your fault! Why are you even here? You are not family! Why are you here?!? I saw the tears welling up in Parris's eyes. As red as her eyes were, I am sure she had already been crying. She was speechless. She had no words. She was beyond shocked that I was addressing her. She stuttered and said, I-I-I-I'm s-s-s-sorry. I told her you are not family. Why are you here? Why did security let you up here? You have already done enough. Why don't you just leave?

My sister tried to calm me down – Ana, this is not her fault. You need to have a seat and calm down. Wait for the doctor to give you an update. After I listened to my sister and sat with the rest of my family, Parris began walking towards the elevator. As the doors to the elevator opened, one of Parris' friends stepped off the elevator and started walking towards her. Her friend put her arm around Parris, trying to calm her down. Parris talked to her for a bit, and then her friend turned to me and stared at me so hard and for so long. I thought she was going to walk over to me and confront me. Thankfully, the doors to the elevator opened, and they stepped inside. I needed to blame someone, and it just so happened that Parris was the easiest target since they had not caught the suspect, and Reggie was at her house when all of this occurred.

I cannot believe Reggie's mother blamed for Reggie getting shot. That witch actually blamed me! I did not pull the trigger, and I do not know 100% who did. I know it was not me. Of course, I am 99% sure it was Raymond, but I cannot prove it since the car was gone when I went outside. Who else would have done it? Who else had a motive and knew that we were at my house?

I am so glad Samantha showed up. Samantha has been one of my best friends and my lifeline for years. We are always there for one another. When I called her and told her what had happened, she said she would meet me at the hospital. Twenty minutes later, she was by my side. Samantha got an Uber to the hospital so that she could drive my vehicle home. She knew I was not in any shape to drive back home safely. As we left the hospital, Samantha asked if I wanted to go to her house or back home to my house. I told her I was hungry and would like to get a bite to eat. Oh, I forgot, Samantha, I have to go to the police station to make an official statement and answer more questions. I am so hungry, though. She said we should go to the police station first, and then we should be able to go and get something to eat. I hope they don't try and hold me there long, getting my blood pressure up.

CHAPTER 37

BFFs Mixed All Up In It

Samantha and I walked into the station and asked for the detective. Of course, I did not remember the detective's name, so I had to get the card out of my purse, which was a complete mess. Here we are at another desk with another receptionist who is unhappy at work. I told the officer at the desk that I had to find the card. The receptionist, Officer Jones, sighed heavily and leaned on her elbow. I refused to say to her what I wanted to say, especially since I was here due to the shooting of my friend and co-worker. Now would not be the time to have an altercation with an officer. I finally found the card. I apologize for holding you up, Officer Jones.

I need to speak to Officer Jenkins regarding a shooting. She asked me for the case number, and I gave her the information. She said, give me a minute. Let me see if he is here. Officer Jones offered me a seat while she looked for the officer and detective. She returned five minutes later and said he was not at the precinct but asked that you only speak to him. Do I need to wait for him, or do I need to come back? She said I can come back the next day. He said he had a few questions for you, but nothing to worry about. I just looked at her. She must have seen the confusion on my face because she placed her hand on my shoulder and said, he told me the gunpowder residue testing came back negative. It does not appear you have anything to worry about. He wants to get some more information. The tears started again, and I told her I would return at 8 am if that was okay. She said that would be fine. Officer Jones would call Officer Jenkins to let him know to be here no later than 8. I thanked her, and Samantha and I left to get something to eat.

After we left the precinct, Samantha and I sat in the car for a few minutes, trying to figure out where we would go and eat. I was hungry but did not have a taste for anything. We went to Outback Steakhouse.

Even though the line was wrapped around the front of the building for people waiting to be seated, thankfully, the wait was only about 30 minutes. Samantha asked if I wanted to go somewhere else. I told her we could have been sitting by the time we decided where to go and drive there. She agreed. We got the buzzer from the server at the podium. Samantha and I returned to the car so we could converse privately. The first question Samantha asked was, "What the hell happened?"

After I told her the entire story, she said daaaayummmm. Then she asked if there was anything I left out of the story. I looked at her confoundedly, and then an angry look appeared. I have never been able to hide my feelings. Anything I am thinking will either show on my face or come out of my mouth. I asked her if she thought I left something out of the story. Do you think I had something to do with it? You know how I feel about Reggie. I would never hurt him or want him hurt. She asked, why does Reggie's mother think you had something to do with it? I don't know why she feels that way. She has to have somebody to blame, and lo and behold, I walked off the elevator just in time for her to blame me.

I had not seen or spoken to his mother since all this happened, so I don't know why she thinks what she thinks. Do you not believe me? Do you think I am capable of this type of heinous behavior? Samantha told me to calm down. I do not believe you had anything to do with this; however, if anyone questions me, I need to know what is happening. I need to know what I am walking into Parris. I told her I knew she was on my side. I feel like I have been attacked and accused of Reggie's shooting, and it hurts me to know that some people think I am involved. I promise, Samantha – I had nothing to do with it.

CHAPTER 38

No Peace Anywhere!

As I started crying again, the buzzer went off. I tried to hurry up and wipe the tears from my face as we walked into the restaurant and handed the buzzer to the hostess. We were seated a few rows away from the bar, not the quiet area of the restaurant I was looking for, but at least I got to have something on my stomach. We gave our hostess our drink requests. While we waited for our drinks, we looked over the menu. The warm bread arrived before my diet Coke and Samantha's margarita. After the hostess brought our drinks, I had an uneasy feeling. I felt like someone in the restaurant was watching Samantha and Me. Okay, maybe I was being paranoid. A restaurant full of people, and I walked up to the podium crying; people would be watching me.

Nonetheless, we placed our order. Samantha ordered a chicken Caesar salad. I ordered a steak, cooked medium-well, a side salad, and a baked potato with butter and sour cream. I told Samantha she would be hungry about thirty minutes after eating that salad. She said I will eat your leftovers because you will only eat a small portion. We both laughed because we both knew she was 100% correct. I consistently over-order food, and whoever I am with has my leftovers as their lunch for the next day. My grandmother always told me," Your eyes are bigger than your stomach."

After the food came and we said grace, we got serious again. We began to talk about what had happened to Reggie. Samantha asked if I knew who did it. I told her I did not see who did it, but I was almost 99% sure it was Raymond. She said who in the hell is Raymond. I told her it was the guy I went out with last night. I started telling her about what transpired at work this morning. She interrupted me mid-sentence. Wait, you went out on a date last night? Not really, well sort of, well, I guess that's what he thought. I thought we were going to hang out after work. Samantha shook her head and told me to continue with the story. So, I started where I left off, telling her about what had happened at work this

morning. She stopped me again mid-sentence and said, so, at no time did you think you were on a date? He said, come on, Parris, let's hang out after work.

Raymond said he knows a bar and grille with good food, and that is an excellent place to watch the game if I want to go with him. Samantha shook her head again. Did you meet him at this spot? I told her no. She asked, did you pick him up? I told her no; he picked me up. She shook her head, rolled her eyes at me, and then said, okay, so you went on a date with him last night, and what happened at work this morning? I love Samantha's honesty, but now is not the right time. Okay, so Samantha, can I finish the story? She waved her hand, telling me to go ahead. I started the story over. So, last night, I went on a date with Raymond, and she said thank you. It was my turn to roll my eyes and shake my head. Reggie and some of his boys were at the spot Raymond and I went to. Samantha's eyes got big. I said, I know, but girl, it happened. I about fell out when I saw Reggie. Then he came and sat at our table, and we – Reggie and I, talked for about 30 minutes.

Samantha said I would have left you and Reggie at that table and let Reggie drive you home. I laughed and told her that was what Raymond asked me – if I wanted Reggie to take me home. Samantha burst out laughing. After finishing the rest of the story, Samantha asked me if I had reported any of Raymond's actions to security, human resources, or at least my manager. I told her no because I only wanted to escape the building. Reggie followed me home to make sure I got home safely. He stayed with me to ensure I was calm and okay. I ignored the smile on Smanatha's face, knowing what she was thinking.

The detectives and officers showed up and practically called me a suspect. They tested my hands for gunpowder residue, asked if I had security cameras, wanted me to go to the precinct to make a statement, and would not let me ride with Reggie in the ambulance. Samantha looked at me and said, you know that all of that is standard protocol, right? I told her yes. I called my dad as soon as the detectives started asking me questions. One of the detectives stayed on the phone with my dad while the officers asked me questions.

CHAPTER 39

Check Please

The police would not let me shower right away. So, I was standing around with Reggie's blood all over me. Thinking about it now is tearing me up inside. What if he does not make it? Samantha said, Parris, stop it! He will make it. His mother won't let me near him to find out his status. I only want to know he is okay. Parris, I know this is hard for you, but you know I am here for you and with you. Then Samantha started clapping her hands and singing the song from Oprah's The Color Purple – Me and you must never part... Shut up, Samantha. We laughed so hard.

I hope nothing happens to Reggie before I have a chance to tell him I love him. Our hostess approached the table, asking if we needed anything and if the food was good. We told her the food was excellent and we did not need anything. We thanked her for checking on us. The hostess came back five minutes later with two drinks. Gesturing towards the bar, she said, that gentleman at the bar wanted to send you drinks. We looked towards the bar to say thank you. I felt the color drain from my face. Samantha gave an air toast toward the bar, and I gave him the peace sign minus the pointer finger. Through clenched teeth, I told Samantha, put that drink down, put it down!

I asked the hostess for the check and some To-Go boxes. Can you bring them ASAP? Samantha asked what was wrong with me.

I told her that it was Raymond. Raymond from last night and this morning? YES! She just stared at me and then back at him. What the fuuuuuu.. before she could finish that word – – I said, yes, that's him. As we glanced at the bar, Raymond smiled, held his glass up as you would do in an air toast, and then winked in our direction. He was just as fine as he was crazy, but his crazy overshadowed his fineness. I told Samantha that if this lady does not bring the To-Go boxes and the check, we will have to dine and dash, and I will come back tomorrow to reconcile the bill. Samantha said it's only been two minutes; calm down. I am right here. You don't have anything to worry about. When Samantha saw how visibly shaken I was, she went to the hostess' station, gave the hostess her credit card, and grabbed a few boxes to put our uneaten food in, which was most of it since we were talking more than we were eating.

CHAPTER 40

Guilty and Flaunting It

After placing the food in boxes and hurrying out of the restaurant, a car pulled up in front of us, restricting us from walking across the parking lot to our car. The driver's side window lowered, and I was not surprised to see Raymond. The evil look in his eyes scared me more than I had ever been frightened before. Raymond said, your boyfriend is in the hospital, and you are at a restaurant with your partner? Your boyfriend getting shot will be a good topic of conversation around the water cooler tomorrow. Better yet, maybe the police would like to see the pictures of the two of you – not even four hours after your boyfriend ended up at Grady - Tsk tsk tsk. I asked myself, how did Raymond know Reggie had been shot and was at Grady? He had to have done it! Raymond smiled, winked, and rolled his window up, leaving Samantha and Me dumbfounded on the sidewalk. After he pulled off, we walked to the car. I am so tired of being a crybaby, but once again, the tears started streaming down my face and would not stop. This time, I think this was a mixture of tears. I had tears because Reggie was protecting me, and he got shot; tears because Reggie's mother blamed me for what happened to Reggie; tears because Raymond seemed to be stalking me; and tears because Raymond had threatened to ruin my life by making false allegations to the police.

Samantha got in the car and asked me if I knew where Raymond lived. I told her I did not remember the address or how to get to his house. She said, I know you are lying – which I was. You don't want me to confront him. All I could do was say a silent prayer: Father God in heaven, please forgive me for lying to my best friend. You created her, and You know what she is capable of. This lie keeps us out of jail and Raymond out of the morgue. In Jesus' name, I pray, Amen. Samantha said, since you do not know where he lives, let's go past the precinct to report what happened.

Samantha suggested I fill out an order of protection to make sure everything is documented. I could not argue with her. She was correct. We walked into the police station for the second time this evening. Officer Jones was still there; she asked what was wrong. I told her what happened, and she pulled up the documents from the DeKalb County website and printed them out for us to fill out right there. One thing the officer suggested I do is get in touch with my supervisor as soon as possible. She asked me if I had my manager's home number. I told her I had an emergency number for her.

CHAPTER 41

Free Advice

Officer Jones suggested that I call my manager before I submit the orders of protection. She said she had seen orders of protection processed and submitted to a place of employment, and the company fired the victim. Officer Jones gave me a victim's card with the case file and suggested I contact my manager sooner rather than later. Samantha looked at me with a look of encouragement. Officer Jones said if he is the one who shot your co-worker, he is not scared to shoot again. I looked at Samantha; she looked at me, letting me know – I got you.

Samantha and I rode to my house in silence. I went to get a change of clothes to stay at Samantha's house. I did not feel safe staying alone. When we pulled to the house, my heart sank, and I started shaking. It looked like a war zone in the driveway. There was still blood, glass, chalk markings where the slugs from the bullets landed, and yellow crime scene tape. I could not believe they did not at least throw the crime scene tape away. I forgot about Reggie's car. I must let his mother know his car is still at my house. Maybe she has an extra set of keys to pick it up. I do not want anything to happen to it at my house.

Samantha took my keys out of my hand to open the front door. I stood in the middle of the living room. The last place Reggie and I were together. Samantha pulled my arm to bring me out of my trance and told me she would check the windows and doors to ensure they were all locked. While she checked the locks, I packed my overnight bag. Since I did not want Samantha going into the backyard by herself, we both went to ensure the gate was locked. I closed and locked the front door, threw my clothes in the car, went to the spigot next to the driveway, and turned the water on full blast to try and rinse the blood off of the driveway. I am sure YouTube will have a tutorial on removing bloodstains from concrete. Samantha told me I might have to hire someone if I can't find anything to clean the driveway.

I sighed and hurried into the car. I sat down in the driver's seat and sighed. Samantha stood outside the vehicle on the driver's side and said, I know you don't think I will ride with you. Get out and get on the passenger's side. You are not going to kill me. I glanced at her and then rolled my eyes. She said, no pun intended. Yeah, that was a poor choice of words. I got out and handed her the keys so that she could drive.

As soon as we started to back out of the driveway, I thought I saw Raymond's car go past my street. I told Samantha to hurry up and go. She asked me what was wrong. I told her I thought I had seen Raymond. It may be my paranoia again, but I don't want to be here if he decides to do another drive-by.

CHAPTER 42

No One Will Answer The Phone

We got to Samantha's house, and I called the hospital and attempted to get some information on Reggie's condition. The hospital would not give me any information since Reggie's mother told them I was not his fiancé. I threw the phone down on the bed and yelled – I HATE HER! Lord, I know You say vengeance is Yours, but your daughter is a little impatient down here. I am trying to hold on and let You fight this battle. I sucked up my pride and called Reggie's mother's phone, but the call went directly to voicemail.

I continued to call her to no avail. I decided to call Reggie's number, hoping he would be out of surgery, conscious, and able to answer the phone. I heard someone pick up the phone, and my stomach immediately dropped. Then I heard her. His mother had his cell phone! I lost my courage. I hung up, not wanting to deal with her disrespect. Reggie had my name and number saved in his phone contacts, so his mother knew it was me. I did not care if she had negative things to say as long as she didn't address them with me.

It was time for me to pray because I was feeling quite a few emotions all at once: Father God in heaven, Your word says in Psalms 91:1-2 – *He who dwells in the secret place of the Most High shall abide under the shadow of the Almighty. I will say of the Lord,*

"He is my refuge and fortress; My God in Him I will trust. You are my refuge and my fortress, and I trust in You. Please give me directions. In Jesus's mighty name, I pray, Amen. About ten minutes after my prayer, I received a phone call from Reggie's number. I answered the phone with a shaky voice - Hello? May I speak to Parris, the lady's voice asked. I responded, speaking. By this time, Samantha had entered the room where I was and sat on the bed next to me.

The lady said this is Reggie's aunt. His aunt sounded like she was whispering. I wanted to let you know that Reggie is out of surgery and is asking for you. I looked towards heaven and said, "That was fast – and thank you." I asked his aunt if it would be okay for me to come to the hospital to see him since his mother did not want me there. Yes, you have time to come. Reggie's mother will not be back until tomorrow. What time is visitor's hours over? His aunt told me nine. I looked at my Fitbit to see how much time I had to get to the hospital. I had about 50 minutes to get there. Samantha looked at me and said, I will get you there, but you won't have much time to spend there. I told Reggie's aunt I was on my way.

CHAPTER 43

One Is The Loneliest Number

I cannot believe Parris left me in this hospital alone. I got shot trying to help her, and she left me. Did Parris have something to do with it? Did she and Raymond plan this? I have been in and out of surgery, and I have not heard from her. I did not see any missed calls or text messages. My mother said she had not called or come by to see me. I thought we had a future together. I guess I was wrong – again. Parris is the second woman that has left me. What is it about me?

I looked up, and our eyes met. Parris nor I said anything. Parris ran over to me. Both of us had tears in our eyes. Parris bent over and hugged me, but a little too hard. I groaned in pain. Parris jumped up and said, oh my goodness. I am so sorry. I started chuckling and tried to sit up in the hospital bed. I grabbed Parris's hand, and we embraced as much as possible. Neither of us wanted to let go. Thankfully, there was a chair in the room. I told Parris to pull the chair up to the bed. She pulled the chair directly in front of me, and we stared at each other. Parris told me she was so scared. Then she held my hand and said to me that she did not want to leave the hospital until I was released.

I felt like the most important and loved man in the world. Parris, what happened? Who shot me? All I remember is you holding me, getting to the hospital, and then waking up after surgery. Parris said, I think it was Raymond, but we do not have any proof. The detectives think I did it. I yelled, what?!? Parris did not want me to get upset and asked that we not discuss this too much. I still need to go to the precinct in the morning to answer more questions. I asked Parris if the detectives could question her at the hospital. She said she doesn't think that is how it works, but she would call the detectives and ask.

Parris, why didn't you come to the hospital with me in the ambulance? It is a long story, Reggie. I guess, being the number one suspect, they did not want me to have access to you, being the victim. When I finally got to the hospital, about two hours after you, they would not let me stay. I told them I was your fiancé, but your mother told them I was not. I left when your mother asked me what I was doing here

since I was not family. She also blamed me for what happened to you. The more Parris talked, the more I did not want her here. The more I did not trust her.

My mother would never act like that or say any of that to Parris. So, Parris, my mother did not want you here? I let go of her hand. She looked at me and said, no, Reggie, she did not, and she is not aware that I am here now. If she did not want you here, then why are you here? I am here because your aunt called me and told me you were asking about me and wanted to know where I was. Parris looked at me and asked, " Reggie, do you want me to leave? I can go and talk to you later. I do not want to upset you or your mother while you are healing. I told her that was a good idea. I saw tears streaming down her face, but until I spoke to my mother, I did not want to see Parris. Parris came over to kiss me goodbye, but I turned my head.

CHAPTER 44

The Perfect Dismissal

WOW! That really just happened. The man I love and could see spending forever with just dismissed me because... well, I don't know why. Oh well. I guess it is time to go home and replay this entire day. The day has indeed been the longest day of my whole life. Almost 24 hours of pure stress, foolishness, disrespect, and fear—too many emotions in a short period. I am so glad I have my therapist on speed dial. First thing tomorrow, I will schedule an appointment with Ms. Tiff. How did all of this happen in one day? It's time to figure out what is next. Samantha dropped me off and went to the store since she knew I would not be here long. Little did she know how quickly she would need to return to get me.

Instead of calling her to tell her I was ready and have her come to the hospital and show out, I told her I would stay at the hospital longer and catch an Uber back to her house. I sat in the café area of the hospital feeling sorry for myself. I could not believe how crowded the cafeteria was this late at night – then again, sickness does not have a time associated with it. I guess the only nasty food at the hospital is the food the patients get because this cafe is full of doctors, nurses, and visitors. I finally saw a few people get up from the table. I hurried over to sit down before someone snagged that table. I pulled out my tablet and began scrolling through some emails.

I opened the Audible app to see if James Patterson had any new books in the Cross series. Alex Cross is my superhero. There are thirty-three books in the series so far. The first book, "Along Came a Spider," was released in 1993. Alex Cross is a detective with the Metropolitan Police Department in Washington, D.C. James Patterson is a brilliant author.

About five minutes into my empty search, I heard a deep, powerful voice ask if the other seats at the table were vacant. Without looking up and with a wave of my hand, I said, no one is sitting there – help yourself. The deep voice asked why a pretty lady like me was sitting alone. I did not respond. He said you can tell me to leave you alone. I finally looked up to see who kept bothering me when I clearly, was not interested in conversing. I told him even if I wanted you to stop talking; I would not be so rude that I would ask you to stop talking or leave. Even if I wanted you to leave me alone, would you? I looked up and chuckled.

I am glad I put my feelings behind me and looked up. This man was so doggone handsome, and his voice – whew – reminded me of Barry White. I momentarily forgot about Reggie's dismissal. Then, the handsome stranger asked me what had brought me to the hospital. Well, I have a friend here. With visiting hours being over, I decided to come down here to clear my head. I dare not tell an absolute stranger; the man that I am in love with dismissed me after being shot outside of my house by a deranged co-worker. Now, I am down here in this cafeteria feeling sorry for myself until I can get over it.

CHAPTER 45

Handsome Comes With The Dismissal

Oh, is your friend (emphasizing friend) okay? Yes, thank you. He is in a lot of pain, but he seems to be much better. The EMTs did not think he would make it so; to have him sitting up and talking is a blessing. My new friend looked at me and asked if my friend's name was Reginald. I looked at him and slowly nodded in wonderment. His question was creepy; how did you know that? I said, what is your name? We have been conversing for over thirty minutes, and I do not know who I am speaking with. We both smiled. He held his hand out for me to shake and said, call me Brandon. Brandon Johnson. Well, it has been a pleasure to meet you, Brandon Johnson. I am Parris Iris. Parris - he retorted; well, it is nice to meet you, Parris Iris.

To answer your question, I was in the waiting room when you came to see Reginald earlier. I heard and saw the commotion. The way you held your composure was remarkable. I told Brandon, I don't know if I should say thank you or hide my face in shame for not standing up for myself. He took my hand, which was now resting on the table.

Parris, I am grateful to have been allowed to express how pleasant it was to see you swallow your pride and walk away. Not responding showed quite a bit of restraint. The spirit of God is shining through you. I don't know why I felt compelled to continue talking to this gentleman, but I did. When I prayed this morning, I asked God for an opportunity to use me so that others could see Him. I did not anticipate it would have been this drastic, but then again, if tests and trials don't come, how will *our light shine before men so they may see our good works and glorify our Father, which is in heaven? Matthew 5:16.* Brandon said he tried to catch up to me, but by the time he got to the elevator, I had already left with another young lady. Oh yeah, she is one of my best friends. We are like sisters. We have been friends for years.

CHAPTER 46

New Prayer Partner

Still holding my hand, which was now sweating from excitement, he asked if he could pray with me. I glanced around the cafeteria, which had somewhat cleared out, and said, um... sure. Brandon said if you are uncomfortable praying with a stranger, I understand. I responded; you are Brandon Johnson, so you are not a stranger.

He lowered his head and began praying softly. Father God in heaven, we place all concerns and worries in Your hands. We ask that Your grace and mercy shine upon Reginald so he can be fully healed and be the servant You called him to be. In Jesus' mighty name, we pray, Amen!!! As I raised my head and opened my eyes, I looked Brandon directly in his face and mouthed thank you, and Amen. He looked at his watch and saw that if he stayed any longer, he would be late for his appointment. I thought, appointment? This late at night? I said to myself, this is none of my business. He stood to clean his tray, then turned around and winked at me. How did he know I was still watching him? I was busted. After he winked, I gave a sheepish grin and looked down at my tablet, trying not to smile as I embraced my emotions from what had just happened the past forty-five minutes.

I was going to call Samantha to see if she was at home. If she was, I was going to leave now. I didn't want to Uber to her house and wait outside for her with Raymond still rolling around. Before I could call her, I saw several missed calls from Samantha and Reggie. Should I call Reggie or Samantha first? Neither of them left a message. I texted Samantha and told her I was still at the hospital. I waited a couple of minutes for her to respond. After she did not respond, I took my chances and called Reggie's number. He answered but did not sound good. I asked him if I woke him up. He said no. Without prying, I told him I had missed a few of his calls and that I was still at the hospital and was sitting in the cafeteria. I dare not tell him I was sitting in the cafeteria with this fine man after he dismissed me from his room. Reggie told me he wanted to make sure I got home okay. His voice sounded so weak. He did not sound like that when I was in his room. I told him I was getting ready to Uber to my friend's house because I did not want to stay at my house. He understood and asked me to see him before I left the hospital.

I did not want to return to see him after what he said. When he told me he did not believe me and needed to speak to his mother to find out what *really* happened was so disrespectful and showed a lack of trust. I refuse to keep reliving humiliation related to Reggie and his family.

After speaking to the detectives, I told Reggie I would return in the morning. He asked me what time the meeting was and asked me to keep him posted. We will get to the end of this. Being swept under the rug is not an option. I asked him if he wanted me to contact his manager. He said yes and thanked me. I told him he needed to rest and that I would see him tomorrow. He said okay. We both said our goodbyes and hung up.

CHAPTER 47

How did the day end with no answers?

I could not wait to get back to Samantha's. This long, exhausting day has drained me. Who would have thought my day would turn out to be so devastating? I am glad Al is with his father and his grandmother in Indiana. I don't know how I would keep my baby safe from all of this foolishness. I ordered an Uber. It was about ten minutes before the Uber driver arrived at the hospital. That seemed surprising; I expected to be a ton of Uber drivers waiting. Nonetheless, I called my baby while waiting.

Hi Al, how is my baby? MOMMY!!! Hi, I am with my Grandma Annie. She got me toys and clothes. I like the toys better, though he said, laughing. Bye, Mommy; I love you. Then he hung up. At least he said he loved me before he hung up on me. Not thirty seconds later, his grandmother called me back. Hi Parris, how are you? I told her I was fine laughing. She was laughing, too. She said she and Al are having such a good time together. I told her to let me know if Al needs anything while he is up there. I would send it to her. She told me not to worry about anything, to enjoy my time alone, and to get some rest. She also told me she loves me and misses me. I told her I loved her and I missed her as well. Little could she imagine how much rest I was not getting. I got the alert that the Uber was 800 ft away. As I walked towards the exit doors of the hospital, I told her I would talk to her later.

I got into Uber and exchanged niceties with the driver. I hoped this driver would not talk to me for the next fifteen minutes to Samantha's house. I enjoyed the music playing on XM – Rachelle Ferrell & Will Downing – Nothing Has Ever Felt Like This – that was one of my jams - the smoothness of their combined voices was so soothing. *Heaven knows, I'm not like you, I'm not perfect. When he sees, will he leave? Or will he stay anyway?* Whew, if I weren't in this Uber, I would be singing this song as if I was trying to win a Grammy.

That was a fast fifteen minutes. We pulled up to Samantha's, and I thanked the driver and got out. Once I settled down in Samantha's guestroom, I gave the driver a five-star rating. I added an extra tip for allowing me to have the only peace I had in almost twenty-four hours. A few minutes later, Samantha entered the room with a Diet Coke and Doritos. My sis knew me so well. Samantha, what a day. She said, I know, and put her arm around my shoulder.

She asked me if I needed anything. I told her an alternate universe; if she can't get me that, I will only need her to stick by my side until all this is over. She reminded me to call my manager and let her know what was happening. She also advised me to take off for the next couple of days. That was not a bad idea since this happened on a Wednesday. I am looking forward to the upcoming four days off. I called my manager and got her voicemail. I left a message that I needed to speak with her immediately. I also told her I needed to use two vacation days. I did not want to go into detail in a voicemail message.

While I waited for my supervisor to call me back, I started the shower. There is nothing like a hot, steamy shower to relax and try and wash the day away. I got out of the shower, dried off, moisturized my face, and used the Nivea Oil infused Cherry Blossom & Jojoba Oil on my arms and legs. I put on my nightshirt.

I took a deep breath, kneeled at the side of the bed, and prayed. Lord God, what kind of day have you given me? I thank You for the angels You have encamped around me that have protected me. Jehovah Rapha, You are the Lord of healing; please heal Reggie's body and mind with no physical or emotional scars. I pray that you keep me safe, and please keep Reggie safe. In Jesus' name, I pray, Amen.

I got up from my knees and lay down. As tired as I was, I was ready to close my eyes and get some much-needed rest. I laid down and got comfortable. As I drifted off to sleep, I heard gunshots. I woke up screaming Reggie's name. Samantha came running into the room. I apologized to her through my tears. She told me she would get some hot tea to calm me down. I am a self-proclaimed tea connoisseur. I was grateful when Samantha brought me a cup of Chamomile tea with a hint of Evans Williams bourbon and honey. I sipped the tea until it was all gone and laid down, drifting off to sleep. Of course, I had nightmares about the shooting and Reggie not surviving. I woke up every hour wondering why it did not seem like time was moving.

CHAPTER 48

On My Way To Play At The Police Station

I woke up at 7 am and began getting ready to go to the precinct to speak with the detective. Samantha knocked on the door; she was dressed and ready to go, and she asked how much longer it would be before I was ready to go to the precinct. I told her I should be ready in about twenty minutes. I asked her what time she had to be at work. When she told me she had taken off, I told her she did not have to use a personal or vacation day for this. You can drop me off at the precinct, and I can Uber back to my house until you get off work.

I told Samantha I could go to my cousin's if I felt uncomfortable at home. She interrupted me and said; or, you can come back here. Samantha, I do not want to wear out my welcome. I also don't want to put you in danger if that idiot is trying to follow me around. Samantha looked at me and said, girl, I got you – get ready to go. I fixed some toast and bacon so you can have something on your stomach. I appreciate it. I got ready and headed downstairs. As the sunlight shone through the recently opened blinds and curtains, my mood and energy boosted. I sat down at the table, said grace, and began to eat.

I got a phone call from an unknown number. I was nervous, thinking Raymond could have blocked his number to continue harassing me. I kept looking at my phone as if I was going to be able to see who was calling from behind the Unknown number telepathically. When I got up enough nerve to answer the phone, the person on the other end hung up. I took a deep breath, sipped some orange juice, and was alerted of a voicemail message. I accessed my messages and nervously entered my security code. "Ms. Iris," this is Detective Ramos. Can you please give me a call? My number is on the card I left with you yesterday. I called Detective Ramos back, and he said he thought he would see me this morning. I told him I was getting ready and would arrive in about ten to fifteen minutes. He said okay, I will be waiting.

I hit the end option on my cell phone, looked at Samantha, and rolled my eyes. I told her his tone sounded a lot different than it did yesterday. He almost sounded angry. Samantha told me to finish breakfast so we could be on our way. In the meantime, I received another call from an Unknown caller. I answered the call this time, thinking the detective was calling me back. Hello? Hello? No one said anything. I said hello again, and the person on the other end hung up. Samantha looked at me and said come on, let's go.

CHAPTER 49

Just In Case I End Up Behind Bars

On the way to the precinct, I asked Samantha to stop at an ATM just in case something went left and she needed bail money for me. We found an ATM at Wells Fargo right off Candler Rd. I got the maximum amount you can withdraw from an ATM. I handed it to Samantha, and we headed to the precinct, which was about ten minutes away. We walked in, and I did not see the officer who had assisted us the night before. I advised the officer on desk duty that I was there to meet with Detective Ramos. She said oh, okay. Is this regarding the shooting that took place yesterday? I told her yes. She said give me one moment, please. She looked at Samantha and said, and who are you? Samantha paused and said, this is my sister. The officer said one minute.

After a few minutes, Samantha and I sat quietly and patiently in the reception area while waiting for the detective. Ms. Iris? Samantha and I stood up. The detective told Samantha she could stay in the reception area and that they would call her back if needed. I hugged Samantha and told her I would give her a call when I was ready. She said she would walk around South DeKalb Mall until I called her. I gave her a half smile and then followed the detective to the interrogation room. He sat across from me and asked me how I was doing. I told him my friend was in the hospital after being shot by a deranged co-worker.

I think the same person who shot him is stalking me. Detective Ramos said I am going to get right to it. There are some holes in your story. I looked at him and said, oh really? Here we go! What holes are in my story that I need to fill for you? I was agitated. I told the detective; I don't care what you think. I know I did not have anything to do with it. Reggie followed me home after I took off from work early because I felt torturous after one of our co-workers glared at Reggie and me yesterday.

The detective asked me what would cause the co-worker to glare. I told the detective that Raymond and I had gone out the night before to watch the game and unwind after work. It happened to be the exact location Reggie and some of his friends were watching the game. I gave the detective the name and location of the sports bar and grille where we watched the game. While he was writing down the name and location of the establishment, the detective asked me if either Raymond and I or Reggie and I were dating. I told him that Reggie and I used to date and that Raymond and I were only co-workers hanging out after work. He asked me when Reggie and I stopped dating and why.

I told the detective things didn't work out. The next question from the detective caught me off-guard. He asked why I told the nurses at the hospital that I was Reggie's fiancé. I told him it was because I wanted to be able to see Reggie. Detective Ramos said so, you lied. I asked if that was a question or an observation. Detective Ramos glared at me, and I glared back. He then asked me why Reggie's mother said I was the reason Reggie got shot. I told him, I don't know, other than being with Reggie when it happened. Have you asked Reggie's mother why she said it? I cannot speak for her.

CHAPTER 50

More Interrogating Questions

Well, tell me about this Raymond fellow. I told the detective everything I had endured since yesterday morning. I told him about the looks we received from Raymond. I also advised that Raymond followed us out of the building after receiving authorization to leave early. Raymond threatened Reggie. Seeing Raymond drive by my house after we went inside. Samantha and I went to a restaurant for dinner, and Raymond appeared at the same restaurant. The detective was taking quite a few notes. I never understood why detectives and police took notes in interrogation rooms. All sessions are recorded and accessible for review at any time.

Detective Ramos asked for Raymond's contact information. I looked through my phone and gave him Raymond's last name and phone number. I told Detective Ramos I had been here over two hours and was ready to go. He said he had a few more questions. I sighed and told him I wanted to leave. I am tired. These past two days have been emotionally overwhelming. Detective Ramos told me I could go, but they would be in contact with me. At this point, I was highly annoyed. What other questions do you have? He said, just a few more. After asking me a couple more questions, he could tell I was getting more and more frustrated, and I answered his remaining questions with deep disdain – I DO NOT KNOW!

I told him that was fine. Let me go and rest for a while. I called Samantha to let her know I was ready. She didn't answer her phone. I was so glad to walk out of the interrogation room to see Samantha sitting in the reception area. I told her, I am ready to go!

We got into Samantha's car. Before starting her car, she asked; where to? I sighed heavily and said, I don't know. I want to see how Reggie is doing, but I don't want to see his mother and deal with her foolishness. After talking to him last night, we did not necessarily end the call on a loving note. He seemed to be a little on edge. I told him I would see him after speaking with the detective. Maybe it would be good to go to the hospital so his mother could explain what she meant by her comment.

One of the questions Detective Ramos asked was why his mother said that Reggie getting shot was my fault. I want her to explain what she meant by that and tell her what that stupid comment did to me. Samantha said, so, to the hospital we go. I just sat back and thanked her. She said, if you tell me thank you one more time, I will put you out of the car. We both laughed. My phone vibrated, letting me know that a text or a call had come in. It was a text message from my manager. She left me a message while I was talking to the detective. I had the phone on silent, so I did not hear any calls or texts. The text message said, Hi, Parris, please give me a call. You are a no-call no-show, and this is not like you. Please call me A.S.A.P.

CHAPTER 51

I **Am Losing My Mind**

I read the message out loud. Samantha said I thought you called your manager. I told her I thought I did, too, but it was such a long day that I may have forgotten to call. I went through my call log and saw where I had actually called. Maybe she did not realize there was a voicemail message from me. I called her back. Hi Sherrie, this is Parris. I am returning your call. She asked what was going on. I told her I needed to speak with her and did not feel comfortable coming into the office because of what I had been through the past two days. Sherrie asked me if this had something to do with Reggie. So, you have heard about Reggie? She said she couldn't give me any information but knew about the situation. I asked if I should speak to her about what happened or talk to upper management or HR. Sherrie asked me to hold on while she got an HR representative on the phone. Sherrie returned to the phone and told me she could not get the rep and that she would call me when she got them online.

We finally get to the hospital and go to Reggie's room. Samantha and I got on the elevator, and I saw Brandon. Well, hello, Brandon; how are you? He said; Now that I see you, I am doing much better, Parris; how are you? I am doing pretty good. He asked if I was here checking on my friend. Yes, I am going to check in on him. Brandon said, well, I guess that means we are going to the same floor. The doors to the elevator opened, and I noticed I was following Brandon to Reggie's room.

I was floored when Brandon slid on his white doctor's jacket and stethoscope. I had no idea Brandon was a doctor. Let alone Reggie's doctor. Reggie's mother was in his room – surprise, surprise. Hello, Ana. Hi Reggie. I looked at Reggie and said, you remember my best friend, Samantha, not remembering if I had introduced them before. Reggie said hello to both of us. I asked Reggie how he was feeling. He said he was feeling okay. Dr. Brandon said, well, Mr. Simmons, how are you feeling today? How is your pain level? Reggie told him the same thing he told me. He was feeling okay. He added that his pain level was at about a 6 or 7. Dr. Brandon told Reggie they were going to increase his pain meds. While Dr. Brandon and the nurses checked Reggie, Samantha and I exited Reggie's hospital room.

Samantha looked at me and said, how do you know "Dr. Brandon?" I told her I met him yesterday. Girl, he is fine, but you know this does not look good for you. Samantha, I met the doctor yesterday when I felt sorry for myself in the cafeteria after Reggie dismissed me from his room. Samantha looked at me and asked; after Reggie did what? I ignored her question and said he heard Reggie's mother yelling in the waiting area and saw the entire thing. He asked if I was okay and then prayed with me. Samantha's mouth was wide open. I told her to close her mouth before she started catching flies. He prayed with you? Yes, he prayed with me *for* Reggie. Samantha said, oh, okay – I saw how he looked at you, and it wasn't a prayer kind of look.

CHAPTER 52

What Kind of Apology Was That?

Reggie's mother came over to where Samantha and I were standing. Samantha said, hello, is there something we can help you with? She looked at Samantha and then turned and looked at me and said, is that the man you were holding hands with in the cafeteria yesterday? I was beyond speechless. Um, well, yes. He held my hand while he prayed for YOUR son's healing. I know that is not what it appeared to be in your little world, but yes, with our eyes closed and heads bowed forward, it was a prayer. You made accusations against me that had detectives thinking that I was a participant in your son's shooting. What have I done to you?

I started to walk away. Ana said Parris, wait! I turned around while rolling my eyes. I looked her in her eyes and exclaimed; WHAT?!?! She looked at me as if she had no idea why I had an attitude with her. She started stuttering and said, I am sorry. I wanted to hug her to make amends, but instead, I looked at her directly in her face, gave her the detective's card, and said, tell him you're sorry! She looked at the card and asked, what is this? I told her it was the detective's contact information. I turned around and walked away.

Samantha and I got on the elevator and pressed the lower level's LL button. We got off the elevator to go to the cafeteria to sit down and decompress. We found an empty table and sat down. Samantha had an enormous grin on her face. I asked her what was wrong with her. She said I cannot believe you. What did I do? She said I have seen you stand up for yourself, but never to that extent. Samantha said she was ready to say something but didn't have to; I wanted to laugh so hard when you handed her the detective's card. Samantha told me Reggie might not ever speak to me again. I told her Dr. Brandon would talk to me if Reggie did not. I said that with a wide grin on my face.

CHAPTER 53

A **24 Hour Dramady - (drama and comedy)**
Leaving nothing out, I told Samantha the entire story of how Dr. Brandon and I met, and she lay back in the chair and laughed hard and loudly. She said so; let me recap: your somewhat boyfriend gets shot in your house – outside of my home - I interrupted; she said, okay, outside of your home; you get blamed for the shooting; you come to the hospital to see him, but his mother would not let you see him; you go to the cafeteria and meet a new man all within less than 24 hours, and that new man happens to be your somewhat boyfriend's doctor? Whew - Oh my goodness, this is too much. This is the kind of stuff you read in a book or see in a movie – we both laughed.

While Samantha was guffawing at my situation, Reggie's mother walked in to get something to eat. She looked in my direction and turned her head as if she didn't see me. At this point, I don't care how Ana feels about me. However, I can go upstairs to see Reggie while she is down here. We picked up our belongings and headed upstairs. As we got closer to Reggie's room, I saw Brandon. He asked how we continue to run into each other. I told him that's a good question. He said he didn't have any business cards with him yesterday but gave me one today to keep in my purse just in case I have any questions about my friend. We both smiled. Brandon added a wink.

Why didn't you tell me you were a doctor here? He said he didn't want to come off as a showoff. How would that look? Hi, I am Brandon, a doctor at this fine establishment. Do you mind if I sit with you? We both laughed. I said, okay, that would have sounded a little corny. I thanked him for his card. He walked me to Reggie's room. When we got into the room, Reggie looked at Brandon and Me. Brandon picked up Reggie's chart and asked how he felt using the new meds. Reggie glanced at me and said obviously, not as good as you, doc, but I am improving. The smile quickly left my face. I looked at Brandon and said, thank you, Dr. Jenkins. I appreciate you praying for my friend.

Reggie, I will talk to you later. I started to walk out of the room. Reggie said Parris, I am sorry. Can you please come back and talk to me? I reluctantly turned around and went back into the room. Brandon was reviewing Reggie's chart while I was telling Reggie about my two-hour meeting with the detectives. While I was talking to Reggie, Brandon left to meet with his other patients. Dr. Brandon told Reggie that he should call the on-duty nurse if he needed anything. Reggie thanked him and then turned his attention back to me.

CHAPTER 54

Insecurity Is Not A Good Look

I am trying to redirect my focus since Parris walked in here with my doctor. I wonder if that is who my mother told me was holding Parris's hand in the cafeteria. I might be making too much of it. Why do I get so uneasy when Parris is talking to other men?

Parris, were you able to get in touch with our manager? Yes, I did speak to her, but she still has to contact the HR representative. I told her I would not return to work if Raymond remained. She asked me if this has anything to do with you. I told her it does. I asked her if she knew what had happened. She told me she was not at liberty to discuss you with me. I told her I understood and appreciated her keeping this information confidential. She said she would contact me once she heard back from the HR representative assigned to this situation.

Parris hesitated when I asked her if she had heard anything from Raymond. She said a lot had transpired but did not want to go into detail. I don't know if it was because her best friend was in the room or because my mother had come back into the room. I felt a little mystified that Parris had not come close to me. Parris did not hug or kiss me when she entered the room. I wonder if it's because she sashayed into the room with the doctor and didn't want the doctor to know we were somewhat together. I will talk to Parris when my room clears to see where we stand.

Parris, how is everything going? She told me everything was fine, but that was all she said. I could not take it anymore. Momma and Samantha, please leave the room so Parris and I can talk. They left the room and closed the hospital door. What is going on, Parris? She asked; what do you mean? You are barely speaking to me. You didn't give me a hug or any sign of affection when you came in. She said she did not like how I dismissed her when she told me what happened between her and my mother. Was my mother incorrect when she told me you and my doctor were holding hands in the cafeteria? See Reggie, that is one of *our* issues. Why is your mother so involved in our relationship?

CHAPTER 55

Insecurity Still Does Not Look Good

Parris, you did not answer my question. Yes, your mother was correct. We were holding hands in the cafeteria. Dr. Jenkins wanted to pray for you! There was nothing other than a prayer being offered to God to heal you with no long-term effects, mental or physical. So, yes, we were holding hands. He saw your mother yelling at me when I came to see you yesterday and felt sorry for me. Did your mother tell you that she accused me of being the reason you are here and that the detective has me at the top of the suspect list because of what she said in front of an entire waiting room and some staff? I gave Parris a look that said I wanted to know the answer, but I didn't want to know the answer. When she told me one of the questions the detectives asked her was, "What did Mr. Simmons's mother mean by, it's because of you, Reggie was shot?" I did not want to throw my mother under the bus, so I looked in a different direction.

I left Reggie's room and looked to my right and left, but I didn't see Samantha or Reggie's mother. I walked down the hall to the waiting room. In the distance, I thought I saw them talking in the waiting area. I know I sound petty, but I hope Samantha will not fall for whatever Ana tells her. As I walk closer to the two of them, they both look at me with an intensity in their eyes that makes me want to turn and walk away. I approached them and greeted them with, Ladies. They both responded with hello. Samantha asked if I wanted her to return to get me so I could spend time with Reggie. I told her no, I was ready to leave. Reggie's mother said already? You all just got here. Yes, we did, but I do not want to be here, so it's time to go. I am not staying where I am not wanted. Hopefully, you will be able to speak to your son regarding what happened when I got here after he got shot. I looked her in her eyes and said goodbye, Ana.

Samantha said her goodbyes and then caught up with me at the elevator. I had already pressed the down button. The elevator could not come fast enough. I had tears rolling down my face as I waited. Samantha did not say anything. She just came and stood by me. My face must be red. Samantha always said when I was upset, and my face was red, she would not interject until I calmed down. Samantha did not ask if I was okay or where we were going. She just stood next to me and waited for the elevator with me. All kinds of thoughts are going through my head right now. Why won't Reggie's mother give the detectives the truth? Does she think I had something to do with the reason why her son almost lost his life? The elevator finally came; as Samantha and I got on the elevator, I asked her to please take me home. She asked me if I was sure I was ready to return home. I told her yes; it's my home, and I am not allowing anyone to drive me away from it. I told Samantha that I had spoken to my brother, and he would help me get protection to keep in the house and have with me at all times. He has gone over the necessary safety precautions of having a weapon in the house, especially with Al in the house. He went over the importance of a gun lock and a gun safe.

CHAPTER 56

9-1-1 It's Me Again

Samantha and I went past so many food establishments. I knew we needed to stop because both our stomachs were talking to each other. We both agreed on Popeyes Chicken and Biscuits. We went through the drive-thru, which seemed to have taken forever. I have the mindset that fast food should be somewhat "fast." We got to the speaker, and since Samantha was driving, she gave the order taker both orders. I wanted a two-piece chicken-spicy, red beans and rice and a diet coke. Samantha got the same thing, except that she got sweet tea.

They had no spicy chicken ready, and we had to wait at least twenty minutes. Also, they did not have any Diet Coke. I chuckled and said good ole' fast food. Instead of Diet Coke, I asked for an unsweetened tea. We paid, got our food, and headed to my house. We got inside and sat down at my table. I asked Samantha if she wanted to watch anything on television. She said no, she wanted to find out what was going on. I looked at her and told her there was nothing more to tell. I have told you everything. I know some things make no sense to you. They make no sense to me, either. I don't know what to do or what to say to make you believe me.

I had my back towards the back door. That is the seat I always sit in, whether at the house by myself or not. Nonetheless, Samantha looked up at me after devouring her chicken leg and said, Parris, then she stopped. I said what is it, Samantha? Ask me anything, and I will answer you. I had not started eating yet. I was hungry but did not have an appetite. I picked up the tea, and to my surprise, it was not unsweetened. I could taste the sugar, and it tasted like they poured an entire sugar container into this tea. Samantha, what is wrong with you? She was still sitting there gazing at me. Seriously, sis, what is wrong? She was not staring at me; she was gazing past me.

Parris, please keep your eyes on me. Samantha started speaking between her teeth, her lips barely moving. DO NOT TURN AROUND! Look into my eyes. I said Samantha, you are beginning to scare me. What is wrong? She said there was someone in the backyard. I said, someone? She said they just hopped the fence into your yard. Again, between clenched teeth, she barely moved her lips and said Siri called 9-1-1. On the other end, we heard, "9-1-1, where's your emergency?" I spoke the address. Samantha told the 9-1-1 operator that someone just jumped the fence and landed in our yard. The operator asked if they posed a threat to us or if they could be just running through the yard. Samantha explained to the operator there had been a shooting two nights ago, and the suspect had yet to be apprehended. We need you to send the police as soon as possible.

Thankfully, my dad told me how to turn my blinds on the bottom floors so they had limited visibility if anyone tried to look inside. We could see a man trying to look into the house. He could not see us, but we could see his silhouette. We were both terrified. We were still on the line with the 9-1-1 operator when she searched in her bag until she found what she was looking for.

I looked at her as if to say, have you lost your mind? She smiled and placed our protection on the table. I put my head in my hands and said a silent little prayer. Lord God, you protect fools and babies; it's pretty obvious Samantha and I are not babies. Please have her return this item to her purse before the police arrive. In Jesus' name, I pray, Amen.

CHAPTER 57

If You Don't Put That Back!

I opened my eyes and saw blue lights coming down the street. Samantha must have seen the reflection of lights in the windows because I saw her slide our protection back into her bag. I looked up towards heaven and said, Lord, thank you. The 9-1-1 operator said, ma'am, you should see the police outside now. Please do not open your doors until they have finished searching your property. You should see the flashlights in the backyard. Those are the officers. A few minutes later, we heard the doorbell. The 9-1-1 operator said the officer was at the front door and it is now safe to open the door for them.

I went to the door and opened it. To my surprise, it was the same officer who came out the night of the shooting. I invited the officers inside. They stood by the front door and asked what had happened. We told them what we saw. The officer from two nights ago seemed to not be in a good mood. He asked me if I had any idea who might be behind this. I told him who I thought it was. Officer Friendly asked me if I had spoken with the detective and given him the information. I told him yes. He told me that he and his partner had checked the back of the house and did not see anything out of order other than the lock to the gate leading to the alley.

Other than that, he does not see anything out of place. I told him the gate door was not damaged. After the shooting, I walked around the property, ensuring nothing was disturbed; the gate lock was one of the locks I checked. He said he would write up a report that would be available within twenty-four to seventy-two hours. The report can be submitted to your insurance company so they can repair the door. I thanked him and asked him if he had time to wait for me to get some clothes so I could go to my friend's house for the night. He told me yes.

I looked at Samantha and made sure it was okay for me to stay with her. She said, don't ask me any foolish questions. Go and get your clothes. I went upstairs and took a deep breath before I flopped on the bed, crying. I could not believe this. All of this because I was seeing but not really seeing Reggie. I am so glad my baby boy is in Indiana. I called his grandmother and asked if she minded keeping Al for one more week. I told her I was trying to handle some business before Al returned. She was so excited to do so. She told me she would keep him as long as I needed. I laughed and said, now, don't make me come up there and have to kidnap my baby to get him back. We both laughed. I told her I loved her and would call her the next day to speak to Al since he was already in bed. I got enough clothes for the next two days and went back downstairs. Samantha looked me up and down and said, I thought you got lost up there. She and Officer Friendly must have had a good conversation because they were laughing like they were old buddies.

CHAPTER 58

Creepers Creeping

As we started walking outside, I received a phone call. Hello? I see you have the police at your house. Was there another shooting? I screamed into the receiver – Raymond, why are you doing this? Reggie had nothing to do with me not wanting to date you. Why would you attempt to kill him? By this time, I placed my phone on speaker so the officers could hear the conversation. I have not done anything to you to deserve this kind of treatment. Raymond laughed and said, so, how is your boyfriend? He is not there to protect you right now, is he?

Raymond laughed again and hung up. I looked at Samantha with tears rolling down my face and said, do you still think I am leaving something out? By now, there were tears in Samantha's eyes, too. She walked over to me and hugged me. She said I am so sorry, sis. I got you. You don't have anything to worry about. She told me to call the detective and leave a message for him. At this point, Parris, you need to inform the detective about what is happening. You have the call recorded on the officer's body cam. It's not like he can lie about anything he has said.

The police turned off their lights when they came into the house. They had the constant blue light on but not the flashing lights. As I walked the officers out of the house and leaned down to pick up my Coach weekend bag, I saw a shadow behind the bush of my neighbor's house. I pretended not to see the shadow because I wanted to alert the officers that we could all be in danger. I asked the officer for his phone number if I needed to contact him. The officer said your friend here has my number. Samantha looked at me, smiled, and winked. I shook my head and got into her car while the officers got in their vehicle.

I told Samantha to call the officer. She said, why? I am not going to seem desperate. I told her someone was in the bushes in the neighbor's yard. I told Samantha that it could be nothing but to tell the officer we would pull out slowly and that they needed to follow us. Samantha called the officer. He answered his phone laughing. He said to Samantha, laughing; I see you could not wait to call me to make sure I gave you the correct number. Samantha was not laughing. The officer said, hello?

Samantha told the officer to follow us slowly and listen to me carefully. I admire the way she can keep her composure in stressful situations. Samantha told him Parris thinks someone was in the bushes in her neighbor's yard. She said Parris didn't want to tell you while we were standing in the driveway because she did not know if the person was armed and did not want you all walking over to investigate and get ambushed. The officer highly suggested that we not go to Samantha's. I don't want him to get away and attempt to follow you. The officer suggested we go to the police department. He would be a fool to follow you all there.

CHAPTER 59

Whose Side Is HR On?

As Samantha drove to the police station, my phone rang. Hello? Hi, Parris, this is Sylvia. I apologize for calling so late; I heard back from HR, and they want to speak with you before you return to work. I know you are supposed to be back at work on Monday; however, you will be on paid administrative leave effective Monday. I had my phone on speaker, and Samantha glanced in my direction with a scowl when she said I would be on paid leave. Sylvia, can I work remotely instead of being on leave until this situation is rectified?

Sylvia told me she would ask HR if working remotely is an option. In the meantime, Parris, you will not miss out on any money or benefits. Just work on getting yourself together. When does HR want to speak with me? Will this be a telephone conversation, or will I have to meet on the premises? Sylvia said someone from HR would contact me and schedule a meeting. I thanked her for her support, and we hung up.

When the call ended, I sat back in my seat, sighed heavily, and waited a few minutes before going to the police station. I took a deep breath and told Samantha I was ready to go inside. She turned off the car, and we both got out. Samantha, are we supposed to go into the station? She said, I don't know. He just told us to go to the station to ensure whoever it was did not follow us. We went inside and informed the officer at the desk that there was an incident at my home, and we were instructed to come here to ensure we weren't followed. The officer at the desk asked for my address. Then, she asked if we had an incident number. I gave the officer the card that Officer Stevens gave us. The desk officer looked at Samantha and me and told us she would be back. I asked if something was wrong. With an attitude, she said, give me a minute, ma'am.

I closed my eyes and said a little prayer. Father God in heaven, I am here representing You. Please allow my focus to be on You so I do not embarrass You and me. I thank You in advance, Lord God; in Jesus' name, I pray, Amen. After another minute, the shift supervisor asked Samantha and me to follow him to the back. We looked at each other and knew this would not be good news. We walked down a long, dimly lit hallway before approaching a group of doors. The officer opened one of the doors, held the door open for us, and then came in and motioned for us to have a seat. This room reminded me of the interrogation room I was in the previous day. Samantha and I sat and listened vehemently to what the shift officer wanted to ask us or tell us.

The officer introduced himself – I am Sr. Detective Moran. I want to know what you both know from the shooting two days ago up until the phone call you made this evening. I asked, what do you want to hear that we have not already told you? Sr. Detective Moran said, start from two days ago; better yet, start from three days ago. I sighed, rolled my eyes, and relived the past seventy-two hours. Sr. Detective Moran said I had an officer shot at this evening after you all called 9-1-1. I need to know what is going on for your and my officer's protection.

CHAPTER 60

From a Fence-Jumper To A Shooter?

I said, what do you mean an officer was shot at? This evening? I started the story again. I began with the night Raymond and I went out to enjoy the game, then the following day when Reggie got shot, and ended with the day Samantha and I saw someone in the backyard, and we called 9-1-1. Samantha filled in all of the gaps because there were some points I inadvertently omitted. After re-stating the past three days, I thought maybe Reggie's mother was correct. Perhaps I am the reason he was shot. Although I did not pull the trigger, I felt responsible for someone pulling the trigger. I immediately felt like I had to vomit.

I grabbed the trashcan next to the desk where I was sitting. Samantha looked at me with disgust on her face. She asked, what is wrong with you? I told her, I feel like I have to throw up. Samantha, chuckling, said, oh, ok, keep your face towards the trash can and away from me. I told her to shut up. We both snickered. My laughter made the nausea worse. I was thinking, am I sick? Have I contracted a stomach virus? Did I eat some bad food? I was thinking it's probably that doggone Popeyes chicken. Who knows? I know I don't feel well. I asked the detectives how much longer we needed to be there. I told him, I think we have given you all of the information you need. My words must have come out sharper than I thought because Samantha turned and looked at me like I had lost my mind. Still keeping my eyes on the trash can beside me, I reiterated, I DO NOT FEEL WELL. Sr. Detective Moran told us we were free to go and that they would be in touch with any updates. He gave Samantha his card this time. He probably didn't want me to vomit on it.

Samantha told me to make sure I did not throw up in her car. I told her I felt better and may have just needed some air. To be sure, Samantha gave me a plastic bag from a grocery store. Thankfully, she had one in the back of her car. As soon as the vehicle started moving, my Popeyes chicken came up. This chick slammed on breaks and asked me what was wrong with me. I told her it was a good thing there were no cars behind us. She exclaimed, oh shoot, you are right; that would have been bad. She pulled into the Wells Fargo parking lot and got some tissue from the back of her car so that I could clean myself up and clean up her car. We proceeded to her house after I was sure I was feeling better.

Dang it! I exclaimed as I got ready to shower. She came running into the room, asking what was wrong. I told her I forgot my pajamas. She looked at me, rolled her eyes, and walked back out of the guest bedroom. I said Samantha, I need some pajamas. Samantha came back into the guest room and threw a nightshirt at me. We were both laughing at that point. She told me I had enough drama for the day; extra drama was unnecessary. All I could do was laugh. She said, do not scare me like that again! I told her I promised and then said; nah, I can't promise that; you know me. Laughing, we gave our typical "I love you, sis" hug, and I hopped in the shower. Samantha finished doing what she was doing before I scared her.

Not long after I got out of the shower, I tried to call Reggie again. Either he was asleep and ignoring me, or his mother had his phone. Either way, I did not get to talk to him before I went to bed. I was so fatigued that I fell asleep quickly. I was only sleeping for about an hour when I woke up screaming.

Samantha ran into the room where I was staying. She asked me what was wrong. I started telling her about my dream. She and I went to see Reggie. We ran into Brandon at the hospital's entrance and, of all people to walk up to the three of us talking, Reggie's mother. She said, did you come to see Reggie or Reggie's doctor? We all looked at Reggie's mother before walking to the elevator to go upstairs. The four of us were on the elevator together. We were walking behind Reggie's mother without anyone saying a word. As we walked closer to Reggie's room, his room moved further away. The faster I walked down the hallway, the further away his room got - the room numbers kept repeating. Finally, I got to Reggie's room, and Brandon leaned on the wall outside Reggie's door while reading Reggie's chart. A nurse in Reggie's room was frantically pressing a button on the wall while the alarms were screaming, signifying that Reggie's status had become critical. The nurse kept pressing the button and saying the button was not working. The button is not working. Brandon was standing there and not attempting to help Reggie. Reggie's mother was walking away from his IV bags while quickly putting a syringe in her purse. I asked her what she had done, and she just started smiling and swiftly walking away towards the elevator while Reggie's monitors were indicating Reggie needed to be resuscitated.

That's when Samantha woke me up. She put her arm around me and asked if I wanted tea or anything to drink. Behind my tears, I told her I was okay and would try to go back to sleep. I called Reggie one more time to no avail. I prayed that he was all right.

CHAPTER 61

Where is Reggie?

The morning took forever to come. I woke up every half hour. I went into the bathroom, and my eyes were red and puffy. It was apparent that I had been crying all night. I tried to call Reggie again, but there was no answer. I want to go to the hospital, but I don't know if that is a good idea. After brushing my teeth and washing my face repeatedly as if that would wash the swelling of my eyes away, I headed downstairs. I could smell the coffee. It reminded me of waking up at my grandmother's house. My grandmother would get up early in the morning and fix her Sanka coffee. She would get the milk out of the refrigerator and get her Sweet-N-Low. I remember it like it was yesterday. The Sanka was in a glass jar with an orange label and an orange lid. I still do not understand why we were not allowed to drink her Sanka even though Sanka is 99.7% caffeine-free. I guess that was just one of the old folk's ways. Back then, you dare not ask why. That was the quickest way to get popped in the mouth - the good ole' days.

Samantha said, good morning, sleepy head. Do you want some coffee? I told her no thanks; the thought of it made me nauseous. I told her I would take some water and a piece of toast. Thankfully, Samantha had a half-bath downstairs. I ran so fast to the bathroom to vomit again. I asked Samantha if she had any reaction to anything we ate in the past few days. She said no and that she felt fine. She told me it was probably from frustration, taking medicine on an empty stomach, and stress.

Since I had not eaten much over the past seventy-two hours, it was dry heaving by this time. After I finished getting myself together, Samantha had a piece of toast and some water on the table for me. I nibbled at the toast while Samantha asked what I planned on doing throughout the day. I told her I wanted to go to see Reggie. I had been calling him all night, but he was not answering his phone. I am not sure when he was supposed to be released. Samantha picked up her phone, found the number at the hospital, and called their customer service desk. She asked to be transferred to Reggie Simmons's room. The receptionist advised that he had been released. Samantha said thank you, hung up, and told me he was released. So, maybe his phone is not charged. She said to give him some time to get situated wherever he is and that he would be sure to contact you.

CHAPTER 62

IAlways Feel Better With A Witness

I looked at my phone and told Samantha to stay downstairs with me because it was my manager. I looked at my phone again to answer it and said, on a Saturday? Hello? Sylvia greeted; hello, Parris. This is Sylvia. The HR rep is online with us; she has some questions for you. Okay. Hello, Parris, my name is Tia. I received your message regarding the situation between you and Raymond. Please let me know what transpired that made you uncomfortable coming to work. I told her in detail what happened. Tia said this started when you agreed to eat with Raymond after work.

Samantha and I looked at each other like, is she blaming me for all this? Yes, I agreed to go out and watch a game and grab something to eat at a sports bar and grille. Did you all have any adverse interactions while you were at the restaurant that would have carried over into the next day? Not really; a mutual friend was at the sports bar. I could tell there were negative vibes between the two, so I tried to talk to both of them to try and take the tension out of the air. When the mutual co-worker came to the table to speak, Raymond said it was okay for him to sit down. I thought we were all okay with Reggie joining us for a few minutes, but clearly, Raymond was not.

Reggie (the mutual friend) bothered Raymond by coming to our table. Raymond thought that was disrespectful. After

Raymond dropped me off at my house, he did not wait for me to get to my door before he left. The next day at work, I was so uncomfortable with Raymond's stares that I left work early. Reggie also took off early to make sure I got home okay. That is when my car was damaged, and Reggie was shot.

Samantha and I looked at each other. They already knew what was happening since neither Sylvia nor Tia responded to my last comment. Oh my God, I exclaimed. I asked both of them to hold on. I ran to the bathroom again and vomited. I should go to the doctor's today to find out what is happening. I rinsed my mouth with some of the mouthwash on the sink; I got back on the phone and apologized to both women. They asked if I was okay. I told them I had been sick for the past two days and may have a stomach virus. I asked them if they had any further questions and what the next plan of action would be. They had no further questions but told me I would hear back on Monday or Tuesday. Before we hung up, I advised them that I wanted to have a restraining order submitted against Raymond. Tia asked why I had not told her my car had been vandalized.

I saw a car that was identical to Raymond's car speeding off. I could not see his face, but when my friend and I went out for dinner, Raymond happened to be at the same restaurant we were going to. As my friend and I left, Raymond pulled up next to us, stopping us from getting to our vehicle. Tia asked if the friend was Reggie. I told her no; Reggie was in the hospital when all of this transpired. It was one of my long-time best friends. She has been with me through all of this. Oh ok. Thank you for clarifying, Tia said before she and Sylvia hung up.

CHAPTER 63

Time To Visit The Doctor

Samantha, I need to go to the doctor to see if this is a stomach virus or something more serious. She started laughing and saying, more serious? Like something you might have to care for 18 years, serious? I told her that was not funny. We got ready to go to the Urgent Care facility on Fairview Rd. Thankfully, there were only two people ahead of me. I made sure to put on a mask just in case it was something contagious. However, Samantha did not have any symptoms. When they called my name, I went to the back. I had to get on the scale, and then the nurse took my vitals. Why is it that the nurses always need to take your weight? I am vomiting. What does weight have to do with that? Samantha waited in the car so that I could have some privacy. The nurse started going down my family history. The nurse's first question was, does high blood pressure run in my family?

I was thinking, I am black. Doesn't it run in almost every black family? I told her yes on my maternal and paternal sides of the family. Does diabetes run in your family? No, not to my knowledge. Could you be pregnant? Um, I smiled and said, I guess that's always a possibility until after I reach menopause – in my head, I started counting back to my last cycle. Oh, my goodness, did I miss my previous cycle? I don't think I missed it. Of course, I do not have my calendar with me to confirm.

The nurse pulled a cup out of the drawer and had the audacity to say, you know what to do. I asked her if I really had to. She said yes if you want to know what is wrong with you. I slowly walked to the restroom, still trying to remember my last cycle. The nurse said she would be back in a few minutes. I texted Samantha and told her they were doing a few tests and that, hopefully, it would not be much longer. Samantha told me it was no problem. She was on the phone with her new Boo – Officer Brian Johnson. I told her bye and hung up on her. I had to chuckle – that's my girl. The nurse returned to the room, holding a fold and a few clipboards. She said, Ms. Iris, this is for you. My mouth was opened, and my heart was racing. Are you kidding me? No ma'am. I am not joking. She handed me a folder and had me sign some paperwork indicating that I understood all the tests given and would adhere to the doctor's orders. My hand shook so badly that my signature looked like a ten-year-old trying to write in cursive.

CHAPTER 64

What did the doctor say?

I walked to Samantha's car. She was still on the phone kee-keeing with Officer Friendly. I thought, now is not the time for any laughter. I attempted to call Reggie again. The phone rang twice and then went to voicemail. Did he send me to voicemail – again? Okay, that is enough. I will not reach out to him since it does not appear he wants to converse with me. I heard Samantha tell Brian she would call him back. She hung up and then looked at me. So, how are you feeling? I told her I felt horrible.

Reggie is still not answering my phone calls. She said, don't nobody care about Reggie. What did the doctor say? I handed her all of the paperwork the nurse gave me. Samantha said, let's go back to my place so you can lie down. You definitely need to rest. Your eyes are puffy and red, and you, I love you, sis, but you look horrible. I laughed and said, I can't stand you. We both chuckled.

Reggie called back about ten minutes after he sent me to voicemail. Hello? He sounded like I felt. How are you? I asked. He said I am doing okay. I was released this morning. I thought to myself, thanks for letting me know. I told him I found out when I called the hospital. I have been calling you. Reggie told me he was feeling better now than when he went into the hospital. Smiling, I said – I bet you do. He said, Parris, I miss you. I let him know I missed him too, but I don't think your mother wants me anywhere near you right now. I cannot blame her with Raymond still on the loose. I can definitely understand her protecting you.

Reggie asked me what I was up to today. I told him I was with Samantha and on my way back to her house. He said he wanted to come by to see me soon. Until Raymond is arrested, I don't want you to be near me, although I do want you to be near me. We both chuckled, and he said, please don't make me laugh. I am still in agonizing pain. I told him I was virtually sending my love to him and sealing it with a kiss. He said he received it and he loves me too.

I asked if he would stay with his mother for a while. He said he would be staying with her until he finishes his rehab. How long do you anticipate having to go to rehab? He wasn't sure, but he said he wanted to see me before completing rehab. He wanted to at least FaceTime me since we could not be together. I told him he did not want to see me right now. Samantha co-signed on that statement. I looked at her and told her to mind her business.

She almost ran the red light, laughing. We got back to Samantha's house. I went upstairs to lie down. Samantha told me that Brian would come over when he finished his shift. I told her I could return to my house so they could be alone. She told me absolutely not. She said I invited him here so that I would not be alone with him. I rolled my eyes at her - girl, what am I going to do with you?

CHAPTER 65

One, Two, I Am The Third Wheel Again

After my much-needed six-hour nap, I woke up to ten missed texts and a few missed phone calls, including calls from the detectives working on the case. I called Detective Ramos back, and he asked if I could come to the station. I told him I was not feeling well. Can we discuss any questions you have over the phone, or must the meeting be in person? Detective Ramos said he would prefer I come into the precinct as soon as possible. Do I need to get a lawyer? I do not like how your tone is coming across. Detective Ramos advised that it is up to me whether or not I get an attorney. He said they only had a few more questions. I informed Detective Ramos that I did not have my vehicle and wanted to know if anyone could bring me back to my sister's house. Detective Ramos confirmed my address from the paperwork in front of him. I gave him Samantha's address and informed him I was scared to stay at my house since no one had been arrested for the shooting or the stalking. He told me a ride to Samantha's could be arranged. Okay, I am on my way. He said okay, I will see you soon.

I texted Samantha to see if they were decent enough for me to come downstairs. Samantha said yes. I went downstairs. She and Brian were watching Life. I sat down for a minute to watch some of it with them. Ugh, I am the third wheel. Samantha, I am out. I will see you all later. Samantha asked where I was going. Detective Ramos asked me to come to the station to answer more questions.

Brian looked at me perplexed. Brian asked if they had more questions for me. I told Brian and Samantha that's what I asked. I also asked if I needed an attorney, and Detective Ramos said it was up to me. Samantha told me she would take me. I told her she was on a date and I could call an Uber. Brian said, well, I guess that's my queue. I said your queue to do what? He said; leave - I know how tight you and Samantha are, and she will not let you Uber. He chuckled and said, thick as thieves.

I reminded Brian that I was on my way to a police station. Can you please refrain from saying anything that is deemed illegal? Thank you; it is much appreciated. We all laughed as Samantha put their dishes in the dishwasher, turned off the television, and got her keys. We all headed out at the same time.

CHAPTER 66

The Last Meeting With The Detectives: For Now

Samantha and I arrived at the police station. Detective Ramos called for me to come to the interrogation room. Samantha stood up with me. The detective said, I only need to speak with Ms. Iris. Samantha said that both of us have information from our encounter with Raymond, so I think you need to hear from both of us. Detective Ramos nodded and waved for us to come with him. I winked at Samantha. I will feel much better with her by my side. We took our seats, and Detective Ramos said, I will come out and say it. I think you had something to do with the shooting that took place outside of your house.

I figured you would say that since you said that before. My response is the same. I DID NOT! What you are not going to do is pin this on me when I have given you the name of the individual I think had something to do with the shooting.

We returned to Samantha's vehicle. She unlocked her doors, and we got in. She looked at me and asked, what just happened? I said; I have no idea. Samantha said, did you say therapists? As in more than one? I responded, yes, therapists, as in my mind needs healing, just like my body needs healing. We get yearly physicals for our bodies. Why leave the mind out of the vital checkup as well? So, yes, therapists. One listens to my issues, and one prescribes me medication to deal with my concerns responsibly. I told Samantha to be glad that my problems have been identified, diagnosed, and are being treated. With God and medication, I will be perfectly fine.

EPILOGUE

The interrogation ended with us no closer to determining what happened to Reggie. I asked the detectives if I was being detained. Detective Ramos told me no and said I was free to go. I thanked the detectives for their time, and Samantha and I stood up to leave. The detectives advised me that they would be in touch with me and for me not to leave the area.

As Samantha and I left the interrogation room, we saw Raymond in handcuffs, looking extremely disheveled. Scouring at me and yelling, I didn't do anything! I didn't do anything! I wondered why they were bringing him through the front doors of the precinct. As Samantha and I walked to her car, we saw Raymond's car door open, and his car was still running. Maybe they were watching him closer than I thought. Samantha and I continued to her car. I turned around, and Detective Ramos gave me a thumbs up. We got in Samantha's car and exhaled. I called Ana to let her know there was an arrest. She thanked me, apologized for the accusations against me, and told me she loved me.

After hanging up with Ana, I received a phone call. It was Detective Ramos asking us to come back into the precinct. I told him we would be right there. I laid my head back and took a deep breath, thinking, here we go - again. We went into the precinct, and Detective Ramos sat Samantha and Me down and advised us that he did not want to alarm us earlier, but they were having Raymond followed, and when he followed us to the precinct, he walked right into their trap. Detective Ramos needed me to identify Raymond and make a formal report. I had not felt this safe in quite some time. I thanked the Detective for keeping us safe and diligently working to get Raymond where he belongs, or so I thought.

About the Author

I am from Washington, D.C., but I grew up in Largo, MD. I come from a family that I considered the norm. I had my mom, my dad, and one sister - so I thought.

At the age of almost 40, I discovered I had a few more siblings from my biological father, whom I never knew. Discovering a different side of you that is almost identical to your beliefs, habits, laughs, and quirks is interesting. Of course, not everyone loved with open arms, but I love them all the same. FAMILY IS FAMILY!

I have a solid Christian faith that has carried me through a tremendous amount of anguish, uncertainty, shame, and sorrow. Even with an Associate's degree, a Bachelor's degree, and a Master's degree hanging on my wall, I never thought I was good enough, strong enough, or intelligent enough to excel in anything other than ordinary. My Lord and Savior put the extra he held in his hand for me with the ordinary I could see. He allowed me to increase my faith; now I see my God-given EXTRA-ORDINARY!